Praise for Addie Tsai's
Unwieldy Creatures

"*Unwieldy Creatures*, unrelenting in its inventiveness and its ambition, is easily the most innovative book I've read in years. Addie Tsai manages to hold on to the useful parts of tradition while creating a wholly original revision of *Frankenstein.* I'm hooked."

—Kiese Laymon, author of *Heavy: An American Memoir*

In this thought-provoking and structurally innovative queer biracial gender-swapped reimagining of Mary Shelley's *Frankenstein*, Addie Tsai examines what it means to be seen as a monster in an already monstrous world. From Dr. Frank's innovations in embryology to her intern Plum's ambitions, these two characters must relive their pasts to understand their role in Dr. Frank's creations—and to realize the ways our greatest human triumphs are often born from our darkest human failings.

—Kelly Ann Jacobson, author of *Tink and Wendy*

"Tonally exquisite, culturally crucial, and a master class in the art of retelling, Addie Tsai's *Unwieldy Creatures* will enrapture any reader who encounters it. Fans of *Frankenstein* will appreciate the way Tsai's deep engagement with the original text underscores Shelley's eternal relevance. But all will be enamored with Tsai's dreamy, eerily relevant re-envisioning. The protagonists of *Unwieldy Creatures* may come to grips with the limitations of their ambitions, but I assure you, there is no limit to what Tsai achieves in these pages. In their soulful devotion to selfhood, the body, and the depths we'll sound in pursuit of connection, Tsai spins an empathic spell that embraces the darkness while imbuing it with light."

—Piper J. Daniels, author of *Ladies Lazarus: Essays*

"Tsai takes us on a wild ride in which gender, race, class and sexual identity collide on a grand scale. Like the nameless creature in Mary Shelley's *Frankenstein*, we are forced to ask, 'Who am I?'"

—Kathleen Alcalá, author of *Spirits of the Ordinary*

"小 籠 包/xiǎolóngbāo/soup dumplings, congee/粥/zhōu, guàbāo/割包/pork belly bun, please, readers, pay close attention to food in Addie Tsai's *Unwieldy Creatures*, and how it exists simultaneously in Mandarin and English, which makes food not only sustenance, but a communicative doorway between worlds and people. Even the protagonist, Plum, who wonders if 'communication with another is the only thing we have to keep us from the darker depths' serves as a communicative doorway—*Unwieldy Creatures*, as a whole, keeps us from darker depths."

—Steven Dunn, author of *Potted Meat*

"While Tsai nods to the original epistolary format via oral history, the resulting Unwieldy Creatures is in itself a true original and a perfect example of a flip from a historical classic to a contemporary one."

—Wendy J. Fox, *BuzzFeed News*

"Two queer scientists and the nonbinary creation one of them makes? Sign me up."

—*BookRiot*

"At once daring, inventive, and bravely told, Tsai's Frankenstein retelling is as faithful to the starkness and darkness of the original novel as to its urgent glimmer of hope. Unwieldy Creatures will appear on my syllabi next to Wollstonecraft and Shelley."

—Rachel Feder, Associate Professor of English and Literary Arts, University of Denver; Author of *Harvester of Hearts: Motherhood under the Sign of Frankenstein*

Unwieldy Creatures

Unwieldy Creatures

By Addie Tsai

ISBN: 978-1-938841-36-1

This book is also available in electronic book format.

Tsai, Addie
Unwieldy Creatures / Tsai
Cover Art by Isip Xin
Cover Design by Crystal Hairston

Published by Jaded Ibis Press.
http://www.jadedibispress.com

A Note on the Cover

Quotations on the cover are from
Mary Shelley's *Frankenstein*.[1]

1 Shelley, Mary Wollstonecraft. *Frankenstein; or, The modern Prometheus* (London: Lackington, Hughes, Harding, Mavor, & Jones, 1818).

for Mary and for all unwieldy creatures

Invention, it must be humbly admitted, does not consist in creating out of void, but out of chaos.

—Mary Shelley

No man chooses evil because it is evil; he only mistakes it for happiness, the good he seeks.

—Mary Wollstonecraft

PROLOGUE

Like all stories, this story starts with a secret, my darkest one. It is not necessary that the secret I held so close to my chest is the darkest one for the world, only that it is so in my heart.

我叫李.[2] If you do not read or understand Mandarin, just Plum will do. At least, that's what Ko called me. And it's the only name that matters to me now. But it is also our family's name, one we share with 李小龍.[3] He is someone who has always mattered a great deal to me, since we are both caught between two worlds. We both share Chinese fathers and mothers from the paperwhites, a connection I grew to understand is rarer than expected.

This is a story of ambition gone wrong. I was warned, and then warned again, and yet, it didn't stop me. 可是[4] maybe my story will help you, even in some small way. At least it's my wish that it will help another not stray so far from what matters. Someone once told me the only way to move on from something is to go through it. By the time I realized how true this was, it was too late for me. I only hope that this letter gets to you in time.

---

2 Wǒ jiào Lǐ—I'm called Lǐ. (Lǐ is a common surname but also translates to plum.)

3 Lǐ Xiǎolóng—Bruce Lee

4 Kěshì—But

李

Maybe I should have given him more credit. Then again, sometimes all it takes is one wrong move to lose everything. So many years ago now, I didn't know how to tell my 父親[5] what I was. I was young, and things were different then. I was convinced he would kick me out into the streets, so better to beat him to it, my black duffel an albatross around my neck, a symbol of permanence. At least this way, I had control over my own exile, my own body, especially after having such little control over anything for so long. I had no idea if I could actually make it on my own, but I couldn't envision a way to stay. I knew he would be 愛面子.[6] My shoulder sagged from the thread of silence spooling longer and longer with each step I put between us. I just couldn't think of any other way to survive.

---

5 fùqīn—father
6 àimiànzi—proud

I grew up in Vermont, a far cry from where I am now, but even years after my self-imposed exile, I can still feel the cold winds schedule their passing through my chafed and raised skin. Who would have thought I'd ever miss them? I've been in the South for so long now it feels part of me, although I'll never get used to the people the South attracts, the lack of distinct seasons aside from a tropical storm or an unexpected cold front. I'm sure I never will.

I left so quickly and never looked back. I have no idea what 父親 thinks of me now, or what he ever did. He wasn't the kind of father who talked about things. I don't know if he lived a long life or died young of a heart attack or loneliness. I made it so that he would never be able to find me. If a child leaves behind their maker long enough, it's hard to know how to find their way back. Despite everything, I hope he lived a life filled with purpose and joy. As I think on him now, the love and rage and joy I feel for him swirls together in my chest like a taut balloon. I guess it's true what they say. Some relationships can never become whole. There's not always someone to blame. I learned that the long, hard way, but I can't imagine having gone about my life any differently. As Ba himself used to say, that's just the way life is. I know what he means now.

Ba never understood what it meant to live in my body. It has always been hard. But who could have known the world would become less tenable with each passing day? Each piece of the body born into my possession gradually taken, the right to do with it what I chose gone without warning, like a thief in the black cape of night. What is a life, after all, without a body to call your own? The body snatchers aren't like Ba or anyone I've ever been close to. The ones calling the shots are the paperwhites (like Ma and her family who neither me nor Ba were ever able to make sense of). At least then they would have been familiar, like the hard ground I slept on as a teen, the blanket of leaves I crawled underneath when the shelters wouldn't take in a girl like me. I don't even know if *girl* is what I'd call myself, but no other word really does any better. So what's one insufficient choice over another? Sometimes language crowds the mind so much, it's like standing without gravity. Sometimes the ground tells you who you are.

Which leads me here. To tell the story of everything that's happened since I first left. What's transpired and what I've learned pushed me out of myself and only left me with more questions. I'm left wondering whether running away was ever the answer. I always thought I'd become a sculptor like Camille Claudel or Martin Puryear, building forms with my body, the dark earth still imprinted under my clipped fingernails. But then all these bodies, including mine, were losing all their choices and I could see what kind of future I could give to people like me or people whose bodies just happened to go "against nature," at least according to the people in charge. The laws these days make me question what the point of art is anymore anyway. Sometimes there's no reason why nature goes sideways. Why would the universe give us science if not to use it?

After a year on the streets, I went back to school, and over that first summer after graduation I worked a three-month internship as an embryologist's assistant at FFI (Frank Fertility Institute), one of the top fertility clinics and reproductive science labs in the country. Wild that it would exist in the South of all places. Those three months were glorious and full of promise, electrified with what my future life could become. At the beginning, my days and nights burst with the little dishes teeming with the promises of little lives.

If Ba knew that I left art behind to pursue one of the sciences, how proud he would be. He would be relieved to know I left sculpting behind, *So impractical!* he always said when I came home from another session at the studio, my dirty fingernails giving me away. But to be honest, working with embryos and forming bodies out of clay didn't feel all that different to me.

In those first few weeks, I wondered if I'd end up back here in front of the glass where I wash and sculpt instead of behind it, where I helped usher future beings into existence. Would there come a day that the prospect of my own future children would fall into the hands of some impersonal technician washing and reshaping my embryos just like I did? Whose hands would hold the course of my own future? Whose uterus would be lined with a question mark? Would it be mine, or someone else's? Would there be an I or a we waiting desperately for an exclamation point? I would, in my own way, end up on the other side of that glass, but not at all like I expected. It is not yet time for that part of the story.

On the day everything began, I trudged through the heat after I had wrestled my gooey legs away from the wood that was damp from the stifling humidity in the air. It reminded me of the time Ba and I waited for 關叔叔 and 關阿姨[7] to meet us at 口餃流鹹,[8] their dumpling house at the edge of Chinatown, before opening hours. We drove forty-five minutes, well, forty-seven from start to stop, from our too-white suburb across town. The sun darkened Ba's arms, which were already a deep beige, as it painted the windows a blinking shade of yellow and spotted my cheeks with freckles I knew made him flinch—yet another reminder of Ma. Ma's white blood was foreign to me, too, even while it lived inside me. I knew, ever since she called me Oriental and refused to take it back, that she would never see my body as hers. Whiteness can be a stronger impulse than the bond between mother and child. And yet, she never had that either.

With a flick of his wrist, my ba popped our seats back to recline as far as they would, and without a word exchanged between us, I knew he intended for us to nap right there in the car in the middle of a strip mall parking lot, like it was something any father and child would do. And so we did. At some point I wound up round and compact, like the little balls of dough I used to shove in my mouth when he would make us dumplings from scratch, my body tucked between his armpit and rib cage. He didn't mind. He never minded. We stayed like that, the heat suctioning us together, Ba snoring, my little mouth a drooling

7 Guān shúshu and Guān āyí—Uncle and Auntie Kwan
8 Kǒu Jiǎo Liú Xián—Mouthwatering Dumplings Restaurant

black circle, until we heard the engine next to us idle before coming to a stop, 阿姨 pointing at us through the window as she giggled at our slumbering bodies baking in the midday sun.

*

As I got older, I became increasingly aware of what I was. I tried to imagine what Ba would do to me if I told him; even in the ether of fantasy, my voice caught in the air, like *The Little Mermaid*, my favorite movie as a girl. It seems so obvious now, but it took years to see the deeper meaning behind its power over me—how many times I rewatched that old DVD he bought at the used bookstore in town, so many I eventually wore it out to the point of disuse. O how I wanted to be that precocious redheaded fish who saves her prince, my imaginary beloved's perfect shock of black hair imitating the waves. In this version of my dream, Ba is pale-faced, with a blonde leonine mane, and a voice as terrifying as in actuality. The prince, in turn, saves me from a life beneath the one I longed for so much. A knife prick in my exposed chest.

When her 父親 destroyed her menagerie of man-made trinkets stolen from the ark stranded in the deep. When the boom boom of his voice rattled the castle. When he with his big, thick hands shook the she-fish's shoulders, tiny and frail, for wanting what he was sure would destroy her. When he finally let her go. When his golden staff transformed her fins into tulle and toes and he smiled like he always knew exactly how to love her. No matter how many times I watched those scenes, they always brought me to tears.

If only it were that simple.

There's no witch in this story, not really, only my memory of his hand, the lines casting his face in disdain whenever I made a mistake, no matter how large or small the transgression. Like clay, the skin remembers when the imprint shifts into a new shape, even when the sting recedes back into memory from air and time passing.

His hand scared me most. I'm sure, after all these years, my secret is obvious, the one that made me take leave of him, the one that put more and more distance between us, the one that made me choose the streets over 割包[9] and 豆花[10] and 牛肉麵[11] and a bed to sleep in. Ba must have known why I didn't cry all those times when he cut my hair like a boy. He only did it because he grew tired of the little hairs jabbing him between his toes as he walked barefoot in the bathroom. The clumps of hair that clogged the drain in the shower. Little did he know he was only making the inside me match the outside. Honestly, it was a relief to see the mirror reflect the only image I could tolerate looking back at me. But that didn't mean he wanted to hear me say what I really was out loud; my razor-lined fade and his hand-me-down trousers that fit me like a glove would mean something. That didn't mean Ba was okay losing face in front of all his friends and co-workers, even if we barely saw them anyway, even if it was *my* face that would lose out, not his. I couldn't bear to tell him this part of the story, to see his heart—

---

9 guàbāo—pork belly bun
10 guàbāo—pork belly bun
11 niúròumiàn—beef noodle soup

the one that might still hope for a daughter, a want he could never confront—fall to his feet. Like 磕頭.[12] Besides, only 爺爺[13] deserved such deference. I couldn't bear to see how ugly I'd become, even to myself, through Ba's two dark eyes that looked back at my mongrel hazels. That's how he looked at me—as though I was alien, a creature that wasn't part of him, either. If I wasn't Ma's and I wasn't Ba's, then whose was I? A question whose answer filled me with fear and despair, one I often avoided thinking about. At least on the streets, I thought, I'd be free. And I wouldn't be alone. I'd have Ko.

At least, that's what I thought at the time.

*

I couldn't hold all the memories—太多了,[14] like a cacophony of sirens wailing against my ears until I was unable to discern one from the other. Just thinking about it now leaves a bad taste in my mouth. It wilts, turns sour on the tongue.

The first time—that I can remember, anyway—I was still in diapers, cloth ones Ba made for me out of secondhand blue and red gingham fabric. I was too young to tell the difference between cloth or Pampers. This is one of the last moments I remember when Ma hadn't fully left yet to chase a dream we weren't part of.

Before she left, Ma told me that when I was an infant, Ba would constantly wash the same two diapers over and over

---

12 kē tóu—act of deep respect shown by kneeling and bowing so low that you touch your head to the ground
13 yéye—paternal grandfather
14 tài duō le—too many

again by hand at the kitchen sink. He wouldn't let Ma do it because he insisted she never cleaned them enough. She begged him to use store-bought diapers, but he refused to spend money on something so wasteful. 太貴了![15] They would often fight about this. It would anger her so much that she would walk out, sometimes for a few hours, sometimes for days on end.

On this one day, I don't know where Ma was. Out, who knows where. Perhaps crashed at a friend's house after playing bridge all hours of the night, or getting high with a man she met at a club. While Ba washed the diapers in the kitchen, he would have me sit down in the bathtub, naked and dry, to wait until the diaper was clean. I missed the fabric cradling my cold bottom as it stuck to the bottom of the porcelain tub. It made me nervous to not be where Ba was. Even when Ma was still around, Ba was my anchor, my ground, my mirror.

This one day, I must have felt impatient. I wanted company—or at the very least, something to stimulate my senses. The sterile, empty bathtub offered neither. Before he could get to me, I'd already climbed over the rim of the tub with my squat, chubby legs and hoisted my little body onto the sofa, pushing six inches of the navy plastic slipcover to the side.

I ran to the sofa too fast. Just as Ba was about to grab me from behind, the diaper slung over his bicep, thickened from working long, hard afternoons in our modest but elegant garden, a white paste of 粥[16] from our breakfast that morning shot out of my mouth and landed on the few inches of exposed

15 Tài guì le—Too expensive
16 zhōu—congee

sofa. I didn't have time to guess what would happen next.

Ba shrieked in a pitch that my young ears could barely process. I'll never forget it. Maybe his scream was a word chastising me, or perhaps cursing my unknowing disobedience. I doubt I was old enough to understand the sounds as words then. He threw me back in the bathtub so that he could quickly clean the sofa without distraction. But Ba had tied the diaper so snug around my waist it left red welts against my skin. This time he made sure the door was closed so tight I wouldn't be able to open it. He didn't come for me until long after my cries, beating out of my chest like some feral creature, had gradually subsided into slow, slumbering breaths. That was how I slowly came to be of the world, with the understanding that my captor and my protector existed within the same body.

李

等一下.[17] Let me start over.

The last night of my summer internship, Dr. Wang, the head of the intern program, and I had to physically restrain Dr. Frank, the owner of FFI, so she wouldn't cause a scene. She's actually the reason I wanted to get into embryo research. I read a book by her I found in the library on a cold night when I was trying to stay out of the streets and keep warm for as long as I could. It was called *The Frankenstein Dilemma: A Future Without Men*, and the way she interrogated how to do away with the need for sperm entirely was nothing short of miraculous. In fact, no one even knew her given last name. Everyone had been told to call her Dr. Frank because she had been determined since reading Shelley's masterpiece and cautionary tale

---

17 Děng yī xià—Wait a minute

that she would figure out a way to create bodies without sperm. Even without that book, Dr. Frank was at the top of her field, absolutely instrumental in changing how we now think of IVF and embryo sculpting. I was impressed, also, to learn she was an Asian queer scientist, in the Southern United States of all places. I would be lying if I didn't admit I hoped to follow in her footsteps.

Even though Dr. Frank was well regarded for that book, there was also a lot of controversy surrounding the kind of science she encouraged emerging scientists to explore. Before getting the internship, I went to a talk she gave. During the talkback, an audience member asked what she thought of the ethical dilemma of designer babies. Similar to what animal breeders do, but of course, made much more complex and ethically ambiguous given the science involved human embryos. A smug expression fell across Dr. Frank's face, as though even the question itself bemused her.

Dr. Frank cleared her throat before she began, adjusted her pristinely starched men's shirt. "Oh, well, yes, of course there are ethical concerns with what I'm suggesting. But one could say that about the entire field of reproductive science. That's why the conservatives have been trying to cut IVF funding for decades. These are new times, and they require new means of innovation, for thinking beyond that to which we've grown accustomed. Men are, it would seem, finally on their way out," she said with a chuckle, as most of the audience and the moderator laughed alongside her. I looked back at the audience member who seemed a bit embarrassed, smiling awkwardly as he returned the microphone to its stand in the aisle and made his way to his seat. A middle-aged man, perhaps in his fifties, pierced the room with his voice. "You can't be fucking serious," he yelled. He said more, but it was unintelligible because a security guard had covered his mouth while another guard grabbed him by the arms and led him out of the room. I wish I had attended with a fellow colleague who might have whispered their reaction in my ear like so many audience members in the auditorium. Years later I would think back to the moment of that man's question and realize she never answered him. I wonder what became of that dissenter. I'm sure there were many more where he came from.

During the last month of my work at the lab, I saw Dr. Wang gossip with the other techs that had been there far longer than me. The whispers seemed to grow louder as ones attached to scandal tend to do. I could tell people were alarmed and uncomfortable with what they'd been hearing. I couldn't hear everything they were saying, but I heard something about a breakdown and her biggest donors pulling funding. I didn't want my idol to shatter before my eyes, but I couldn't help being curious about what was behind all the whispers. All I knew was something was clearly wrong with Dr. Frank, and I wasn't altogether sure I wanted to know what it was.

And then, on the last night of my internship, as we were wrapping up for the night, Dr. Frank blew into the lab like a rash, wild-eyed and pink-faced, her perfectly coiffed hair as frazzled as what seemed to be her state of mind. Her outfit, as always, was elegant and well tailored. She wore a deep violet suit with a bright green men's shirt. The shirt was untucked, and her thin floral necktie was a bit off-kilter, one of the few signs, other than her unkempt hair and complexion, that something was off.

Dr. Wang acted fast. She untied her lab apron and threw it to the side. I followed suit. She gestured to me to hold down Dr. Frank's right arm while she held her left. Initially, I was a bit caught off guard that Dr. Frank didn't make any move to resist us. Her teeth clacked against one another and her skin was frigid to the touch and remained so, even after we walked her outside in the blistering southern heat. Not a drop of sweat gathered on her skin. I have to admit, even as I tried to maintain my composure, I was unnerved by her freezing skin, the accelerated speed at which her eyes darted back and forth. Like someone on the verge of a mental break. When living on the streets as a runaway teen, you learn a thing or two about how little it takes for people to snap. Whatever was going on, she wasn't well. She kept looking behind her, and I couldn't be sure if she was itching for someone to find her or petrified that they would. I didn't have enough information myself to make any kind of assessment about whether it was rightful suspicion or a paranoid delusion. Or both.

Dr. Wang gripped her hand as I finished locking up the lab, securing it with the code on the keypad and my thumbprint. We walked her straight to the bathroom in the pub down the street, threw some cold water on her face, and wet her hair back. Dr. Wang took both Dr. Frank's hands into hers a bit awkwardly, as it was obvious their relationship hadn't yet earned this kind of intimacy.

"Breathe," Dr. Wang commanded, forcefully rubbing her fingers with Dr. Frank's.

"But, you don't understand. I have to get out of here. It could be anywh—" Dr. Frank began in a heightened, accelerated tone of voice.

"Listen to me," Dr. Wang started, then stopped. She walked over to each of the bathroom stalls, squatted to look underneath to ensure no stall was occupied.

"Look. I'm not saying I don't believe you. Everything I've heard, who knows what's true. But whatever you're referring to, it's not going to come in here, that's for sure. And out there, anywhere around the lab, you don't . . . you know, people are talking. You're already losing donors because of the rumors. No one's going to give their money to a queer woman of color who might be going crazy. In the South. You know this more than I do. Okay?" Dr. Frank didn't nod, but she didn't interrupt or protest. Dr. Wang continued. "This is what I think we should do. How about you go home with Li, the intern? She's wonderful and I guarantee you have her utmost discretion. I'd take you with me, but, you know, I have kids and a partner at home. Let's get a bite to eat first because I think food might calm you down a bit, and also so as not to arouse suspicion. Then Li will take you to her apartment, where you can get some rest, and we can discuss everything else in due time. I doubt whoever is following you will know to look for you there."

Dr. Frank's breathing had slightly slowed by this point.

She took her hands away from Dr. Wang's and placed her left in her suit coat pocket, as always, while the other smoothed down her wet hair. She nodded. Dr. Wang, very much in charge, led us out of the bathroom.

Dr. Wang was right. If she'd stayed in the lab in that state, a tech or a janitor would most likely have reported her. Who knows where she would have ended up? Maybe they would have called the police, had her arrested, or even institutionalized. A great mind like hers? What a fucking tragedy that would be. Like Claudel sequestered just as she hit her prime. Not on my watch. At least, not if there was anything I could do about it.

Dr. Wang tried to normalize things at dinner. She introduced us, told Dr. Frank about the work I had been doing. Over a comforting meal of burgers and ciders her brown face began to recede back to its normal shade, and her chestnut brown hair, just a touch or two lighter than mine, resumed its usual relaxed position as it gradually dried and fell away from her face. But she still didn't utter a single word.

After dinner, we caravanned in two cars to my apartment. The lab had furnished me with a generous stipend that allowed for comfortable housing. I'd already paid through the next month, since I was still debating my next move (and honestly, hanging around in the hopes FFI would take me on in a more permanent capacity). And so it was that I took care of Dr. Frank, my superior and my idol, for the next few days as she slept on my pullout sofa. I tried to offer her my bed, but she refused with a vigorous shake of her head. I fed her 小

籠包[18] and 牛肉麵[19] I'd picked up earlier that day from a local dumpling house and offered her constant water and cocooned her in blankets in hopes it would ease the chill determined to rest in her bones.

At times I inquired about Dr. Frank's level of comfort or if she had finished a mug of tea or a bowl of soup I'd offered her. She just nodded or shook her head accordingly. After a few days, the initial wildness in her fell away little by little, and she finally began to look like the version of her I was most familiar with from afar, on those rare occasions when she would breeze through the lab with prospective donors or from the many videos I watched of the talks she gave around the world. The warmth returned to her cheeks. After asking for her permission, I touched her skin to check for a fever or prolonged chills. I was pleased its temperature no longer made me recoil inwardly in shock.

On the fifth day, she finally spoke for the first time since Dr. Wang had silenced her panic-stricken cries. I was so eager to talk to her (but also somewhat hesitant to ask what it was that had transformed her into such a frenzied, distressed creature), that initially I only viewed her from my own obsessively inquisitive lens. After all, this was my chance to ask the person I admired most in the world anything I wanted. When would I get that exposure to an expert like Dr. Frank again? I asked about her research, and she seemed relieved by the opportunity to speak about it.

---

18 xiǎolóngbāo—soup dumplings
19 niúròumiàn—beef noodle soup

After so many days of absolute silence, I was struck by the smooth eloquence with which she spoke and moved by how forthcoming she was with her ideas and research—what led her to her field of study, how she developed her game-changing hypothesis. I, on the other hand, became so starstruck I could barely get words out fast enough as I tried to shove fifty words at once out of my awkwardly small mouth. Inadvertently, my sentences were accompanied by an agitated stutter. 哇塞![20] She smiled gracefully as I stumbled over myself in excitement and fervor, responding as though I were her colleague and not an awkward fan geeking out. It felt like a dream come true, and yet, at times, it felt selfish and narcissistic to only consider what knowledge I could gain from someone so clearly in pain.

She asked me about my own studies, and even though Dr. Wang had told her all of this when we first met, I didn't mind refreshing her memory. She seemed particularly intrigued by my being a runaway teen, an aspect of my story not even Dr. Wang knew and one I didn't anticipate revealing so quickly. She was very curious to hear how I transitioned from the streets to such a prestigious position. I could tell it sparked something in her that related to whatever she currently grappled with, but I tried not to pry. Eventually, though, leaning towards me with an elbow on each knee, Dr. Frank forced my hand.

"You've been very sweet not to meddle in my affairs, especially given how generous you were to offer your wonderful

---

20 Wàsài—Wow

home as my hiding place, but I can tell you're dying to know what's behind my peculiar behavior and exactly what I'm hiding from. I'm no fool—I know everyone in the lab is talking about me. Scientists try to act above such pettiness, but they gossip just as much as the next person. Maybe even more," she smiled, looking directly into my eyes with a candor I hadn't seen her express thus far, and gave me a little wink. The wind I held tight inside me collapsed as though I'd been holding my breath for days. I cleared my throat, unsure of how to respond.

"Yeah, well. I mean, of course I've heard little whispers here and there, but I try to just focus on my work and move on. But, please. If you want to talk about what's going on for you, I'm happy to listen." I placed my hand on her knee in a somewhat forced attempt to offer compassion instead of voyeurism. She smiled.

"I do want to tell you my story. If for nothing more than to warn you, for I feel there is something in our stories—what I can intimate of yours at this point, anyway—that unites each to each. Maybe the only good that can come of what happened to me is its potential to help another, like you. I can see that dangerous twinkle in your eye already. It would mean something to me if I could at least save a fellow scientist and an inquisitive mind like yours from a future of torment." I giggled out of recognition.

"This is no laughing matter. But, oh, I remember what it was to be you. So young, headstrong, the world at your fingers. You don't know what I mean yet. But I think you'll see, once I tell you all there is to say."

I was puzzled by her introduction to whatever she was preparing to tell me. It was ominous, but like she said, I was young, naïve, and too full of the elixir of ambition to even guess what she was hinting at. Now it was her turn to reach towards me. Her eyes returned to a bit of their earlier wildness as she tried to implore me to receive what she would divulge. I also felt that with the intensity of her gaze she was testing me as well, trying to see if I could handle it. I did my best to return her gaze, but I was so enthralled by her that it was hard to focus once I felt the skin of her hand. A soft tingle of electricity shot up my arm, but I tried to appear as nonchalant and earnest as possible. I couldn't help but want it to mean something, that I was special enough to be touched, that only I was privileged enough to hear her story. After Ma, after Ba, after Ko, it was hard not to find myself drawn to her, if only because someone as important as she seemed drawn to me. It didn't occur to me *not* to get ahead of myself, to even wait to hear what she had to tell me before riding that train of hope and anticipation—I knew what I wanted it to mean. Rookie mistake.

Dr. Frank excused herself and left the room. My heart dropped to my stomach as I assumed I had ruined everything with my insecurities and pride, my one chance to connect with my idol. Before I could sink too far into my own self-shaming, she returned with an old tape recorder and a box of unused cassettes, still protected in their shrink wrap.

"I want to tell you the entire story. If anything happens to me, promise me that you will share my story with the world." I nodded solemnly.

That's when she began to tell me what happened to her, a story so akin to my own—and yet which took turns so frighteningly separate—that I feel I have no other recourse but to share it. Besides, there's no way to tell my story without telling hers, too. Just as she did all those years ago, now I, too, feel compelled to share it in hopes it will keep others from the choices that took me down my own foreboding path. Perhaps communication with another is the only thing we have to keep us from the darker depths of fate.

VOLUME ONE

Z

Like you, I'm also a Venn diagram of blood and body. I was born in West Texas by a white man and a brown woman from Jakarta. My father was an oil man—I know, right?—and his father, and his father, and his father. They all came from Texas, and even though I enjoyed my childhood in certain ways, I still wanted to get out as quickly as I could. Perhaps you can relate. What twist of fate is it that I would end up back in the South? Nature is a funny thing, and home is still home whether you want it to be or not, I suppose.

My father was one of those typical white male species imbued with devilish beauty and fetching looks that tend to go hand in hand with predation. Like a serial killer or a cult leader who captures so many white women as prey because their victims just can't believe someone that good looking can be so monstrous until too late. Just a hair over six feet tall, his eyes two milky pools of periwinkle you could swim in to discover or lose yourself. He was naturally athletic, as men like that often are, and long and lean and could eat whatever he wanted without worry he would add even an inch to his Adonis frame.

My maternal grandmother cleaned houses and tended gardens for the richest in Indonesia, and by the time my mother was ten, her skin had already become a mixture of burnt umber and taupe from the sun that beat through her flesh, the heat that etched lines into the back of her neck as she bent over orchids, watering their radiant white blooms, stars against the expanse of lush greenery.

As a child, my mother learned quickly how the different class levels in Indonesia read one another through the many shades of brown as she worked outside with her mother in houses palatial in scope, homes she never dreamed she'd inhabit one day. For the darker your skin is, the lower on the class strata you appear: It is more probable you work in the fields or outside. That's why so many Asians end up wanting to look like the paperwhites—that's the word my mother always used for the pale among her, the ones who were either the color of light sienna because they had money and didn't have to work outside like her family, or the whites that had migrated to the island to live out their retirements in paradise, flaunting the ease with which they performed the native in their Western-marketed silk sarongs and kebayas as they enjoyed Sunday brunch downtown. *Must be nice*, Ma often thought to herself, watching as they shielded their pale skin from the hot tropical sun in their air-conditioned cars while she and my grandmother toiled, kneading the dark soil in their fingers or forming circles with vinegar on the linoleum with their whole hands, crouching along on their knees.

My mother named me Zoelle, an Arabic name that signified a shining light. I've often wondered about the human obsession behind naming things, but lately I've grown more reflective about my mother's particular motivation behind my namesake, whether her hope for my future successes endowed me with a blessing or a curse. But, there is time later to tell that part of the story. The privilege to name is a power in and of itself. I suppose that's why I renamed myself Dr. Frank. It wasn't only its obvious connection to Shelley's novel, a book that meant much to me, that informed how I conceived of creation and began my life's work. It was also a way to remind myself that what I wanted, most of all, was to live an authentic life, straight and singular in purpose. In some ways, though, it is that stubborn insistence to only consider one path forward that's caused me the most damage. Too late to go back now, I guess. I also wanted to make sure my family could never find me. That didn't quite end up as I had planned.

Well. Back to my father. So my father, and my father's father, and so on, for as far back as oil had been a pursuit that led one to endless riches, were all oil men. Part of the lineage I inherited was inevitably born from not only this obsession with financial riches, but also this unthinking need to consume the earth, no matter the human cost.

My father found himself traveling to Jakarta when some Malay executives who expressed interest in importing oil from the United States reached out to my father's company. They always sent my father to close the deals because he knew how to persuade others in a way that they didn't even realize they were being seduced by him. Something inborn; it can't be taught. One dinner meeting took place at the residence of the top oil tycoon in Indonesia. As it happened, my mother helped my grandmother manage the residence for many years. Having an intuition that my father would find her *exotic* beauty appealing, the tycoon asked my mother to cook and serve the dinner party.

As he knew this was no ordinary evening—much was riding on my father's response to this business deal—the tycoon arranged for my mother to dress the part, providing her with a sarong woven with silk the shade of marigolds so fine as had never embraced her body before. He hired another woman to style her thick, black hair, pulled away from her forehead with a bejeweled headpiece affixed with pearls and agate, adding just a hint of creamy powder and rouge on her cheeks, a smudge of kohl lining each eye. Like drinking an elixir, the evening infused my mother's veins with its hallucination of a life away from the toiling of labor and struggle. She reveled in it, even if it were only for one night, sinking into the fairy tale she knew she would never inhabit beyond this evening. After all, yellow-haired princes don't come for dark-complexioned girls like her, with skin thick and taut from all her long hours stripping the floors of its memories of past lives, hands covered in calluses and permanently tinged with the scent of bleach and ammonia, the dark, crusty soil coating the undersides of her fingernails. But even as a teenager, my mother was proud of the life she had built with my grandmother, whom she deeply loved, and had no complaints. She had long made her peace with the life for which she was destined.

Then suddenly, from this one night, my mother's life (and mine, although I didn't exist yet) changed forever.

As the tycoon predicted, my father couldn't take his eyes off of my mother. He drank as fast as he could from his glass of wine and dark sweet coffee, deliberately dropped his napkin on the floor several times in a row so there would be a reason for her to wait on him again and again, offering another opportunity for him to inhale the sweet scent of jasmine oil on her neck that lingered in the air each time she bent down to retrieve his fallen napkin before retreating to the kitchen to fetch him a new one. The tycoon looked on the scene with satisfied bemusement and offered to arrange a private meeting for my parents the following evening. My father undoubtedly was pleased to get my mother alone and all to himself without distraction. My mother, who was no fool, knew this meeting could lead to a marriage proposal, but most importantly, that it could give her a chance at the kind of life in which her future child would have the world at her fingertips, a chance for her mother to live out the rest of her days in comfort and rest. To my mother, it was a small price to pay. Or, so she imagined. As she lay in bed that night while her mother softly snored beside her, my mother dreamed about the businessman's eyes, those deep blue pearls. Despite herself, she'd become hypnotized by his white beauty and all it promised, the gifts she was convinced would await her in this new life. It would take time to uncover all the darkness lying behind the illusion of immaculate perfection.

My father was very successful by the time he met my mother, and there existed quite a considerable age gap between them: Ten years, maybe more. He must have been close to thirty by then (my parents were always very evasive about their respective ages, but I was able to discern a guess from other details they presented when asked nonchalantly enough). My mother was still a teenager when they met, but old enough to be considered marrying age in Indonesia. In Jakarta she'd grown accustomed to stories she heard when she and her mother went to the market for the week's meals about marriages arranged for convenience and financial security by the families of the bride and groom, typically in less modern cities. In fact, in rural Indonesia it was far more unusual to hear of a love marriage—typically, love happened only by accident in arranged marriages, a circumstance that developed after a couple cohabitated and raised children together long enough to *grow* on each other. My father was an American, and to my mother, and most born and raised in Indonesia and Malaysia, living in America was the pinnacle of ambition. It was where, if you were unfortunate enough to land in my mother's station in life (or its equivalent), you hoped to eventually find yourself. All my mother knew was that this marriage would afford her family everything it could ever want and assure her children would be comfortable and successful long after she and her mother took their last breaths. It was through the American world of independence and fortitude my mother would learn the land of riches and dreams didn't apply to everyone, especially foreigners in a borrowed land.

The evening after the night my parents first met, the tycoon arranged for my mother (styled again to perfection, paid for by the tycoon) to meet my father at the tycoon's private jet. Just the two of them and the tycoon's own personal pilot, and my parents were off on a quick jaunt to Singapore, where my parents strolled the hawker center, and my mother enjoyed a feast of her favorite Malay and classic Chinese dishes with a Singaporean twist—chwee kueh, steamed rice cakes topped with dried shrimp and garlic; rojak, a sweet and sour salad with a fried bread topped with shrimp and satay sauce; and a Singaporean take on biryani. My father had been in the oil business long enough to know the way to my mother's (or any Asian woman's) acceptance of his potential wedding proposal was through her belly's predilections.

When my father asked my mother questions about her family and her childhood, like a flower beholden to the sun, my mother would bow her head demurely as she told him about how her mother taught her to cook and clean and garden and work her hands towards a purpose of providing for her home where she lived a simple life with her mother. She told him about her mother then, how she hoped one day she could work enough hours so her mother could rest her aching joints without worrying where the rice for their daily meals would come from, enough hours to make the fish they seldom bought to calm the rumble in their bellies a regular occurrence instead of an occasional luxury. My father nodded, taking in all the details my mother provided as he calculated in his head the risks and rewards of such an investment. My mother didn't include anything about her hobbies or other interests, like the portraits and landscapes she brought to life with watercolor on her rare days off, the weekly Malay calligraphy practice she cultivated each week as meditation. She knew the American wasn't interested in anything other than what she could offer as a dutiful wife. He smiled at her ravenous appetite, the way she demurely covered her mouth while answering his questions as bits of prawn and juices rebelliously fell from her mouth. By the time the wheels of the jet connected with the concrete runway back in Jakarta, the constellations swimming in the hot black sky, my father had made up his mind to ask for my mother's hand in marriage. There was no doubt in his mind she would accept.

The following day, my father and the tycoon met for brunch at a restaurant in town, where they could finish negotiations regarding the business deal my father had traveled such a long distance to conduct with him. But, as the tycoon had hoped, now my father had a slightly different wager in mind: He would ask for my mother's hand in marriage as part of his bargaining currency. My grandfather had died of lung cancer when my mother was a young child, so there was no one else from whom to seek permission. Certainly no one believed my grandmother held such authority, since, as he saw it, she also owed her future livelihood to the tycoon.

Having agreed to the exchange of business and marriage, the deal was done. My father extended his trip to tidy up some loose ends, and within a week, both my mother and grandmother began to pack the few possessions they couldn't bear to leave behind, preparing to join my father on the long voyage to Texas.

李

I heard a familiar tinge in the words Dr. Frank used to describe how her mother was pulled into her father's orbit by those two blue pearls, reminding her of gazing into the eye of the ocean. I thought about all the space between her story and mine, how Ba and Ma met, all that he was never able to tell me about my own lineage and history.

My ba never told me much. I was still clutching my favorite ratted teddy bear to my chest when Ma left with a simple duffel while he was finishing his rounds at the emergency clinic. She knew how long he'd be gone, at what point in the night he'd return home too beaten down by the night's work to chase after her. It's a trick I learn later, when I leave him, too. The night she left, she didn't even call a babysitter to stay with me. Actually, it hasn't occurred to me until now that I'm the second one to leave him, how my running away must have called back Ma, too—leaving in the middle of the night just like she did while he was out working to provide for me. The guilt grips me like his hand on the back of my neck. At the time, it was too hard to think of how he would feel at my leave-taking. I could, instead, only think of my survival.

Just after Ma left, Ba caught me weeping into my hands in the middle of the night. He lashed out, his dark eyes piercing through my skin, like his hands.

"If you want go find your mother, get ready be on the street," he said. I was still only a child. I couldn't obey him fast enough. My small body still trembling, my voice caught in the back of my throat, whimpering little whimpers. I would soon learn that if I didn't keep my cries under control and away from his perked-up ears, it would be yet another opportunity for his hand to strike my flesh into obedience. Soon enough, I silenced every desire, every grief. Little did he know I'd end up there anyway, with or without a ma to roam the streets to find.

But, there are some things I still remember about her, despite how hard she tried to erase herself from my memory. I remember her eyes, the white and the blue conjoined together like the thickened moody sky just before the crack of lightning breaks through, a hot spark in a pan on the gas stove. I'm sure Ba must have felt that electricity in her eyes, too. So hard to resist.

There were times I contemplated looking for her. Did she live alone? Or did she find a new family to love, maybe a man as white and irresistible as she was? Was Ba the reason I didn't have a mother? When I was on the streets and things got really bad, I fantasized about finding her: She takes me into her arms, grabs my torn bag and filthy clothes. We rent a hotel room for the night, where I finally bathe the stink of the street off my skin. She takes me to a local diner for a burger and fries, and then drives me to our home, a lovely, simple house that's the perfect size for the two of us. Shutters on the windows, a porch swing, a tree in the front yard. Picture perfect.

But, I knew better. Or perhaps I was too afraid to uncover yet another rejection. I never did look for her. There is a comfort in holding onto her in memory—Ma's auburn hair falling in long waves down her back, curvy like a snake, but soft and squishy like her paperwhite belly that I used to rest my head against as I slumbered—because she can't ruin it for me.

Ba was so far away from all that he knew, his family and friends and even his birth language, from Taiwan, but Ma was so far away from her home, too. I always wondered if it was loneliness they both felt for home, away from and within it, that made him think that, maybe, they could find their way to understanding one another. At least, I imagine that's what Ba hoped for that first night where they crashed against each other with the heat bodies make when what's most strange can also fill you with the most desire. Ravaged and feverish, an episode you don't think through too carefully or it might all just fall apart.

Once, when I had started high school and we had begun to learn about the dark stain of racism, I tried to talk to Ba about the two warring bloods in my body, to ask him how it felt to be with a paperwhite like Ma.

"Oh, I wish I think about this more," he said frankly, his glasses falling down his sweating nose as he quickly glanced up at me to see if I was serious or if I was just asking a question from my homework. He never said much. He went back to reading the paper, and I went back to my schoolwork. But I knew what he meant. That he wished he had reminded himself what it would mean, her white skin. Not just for her, but for me. To have a child navigate the world split between immigrant and master. But there was no time.

"It was different time then, and then you were surprise," Ba said without looking up from his reading.

I knew him well enough to know what he meant. Before it even occurred to him to ask that question, I had already started to sprout in Ma's belly. By then it was too late.

Z

But, let me go back a second. Before they left Jakarta, my parents wed one another in a lavish Javanese ceremony.

My mother's family isn't Javanese, actually—they're a hybrid of Chinese and Malay—but my white father had read in a local paper about all the different Javanese wedding rituals and became quite captivated by them. Once he got it into his head he wanted that for himself, just as he had with my mother, he couldn't be dissuaded. My mother would learn later that my father always got what he wanted. If he didn't, someone would pay for it.

At first, my mother was incensed—she found it incredibly disrespectful to take on the traditions of a culture outside of their own. She knew what the local Javanese (and everyone else) would think of her, and the very thought of it riddled her with shame. When the tycoon first informed her of the kind of ceremony she would have with my father, my mother nodded obediently without saying a word, glancing at my grandmother out of the corner of one eye. My grandmother, who knelt by the front steps, watering the lush succulents that curled their fingers around the front of the house, looked back at my mother stealthily, a silent knowing exchanged between them.

My mother held her tongue, waiting to express her disdain about the wedding plans until after they returned to their little apartment that evening after a long day's work and had finished their simple meal of chicken broth poured over a small bowl of rice.

"Ma, I can't do this wedding. It's wr—" my mother started to say in Indonesian. Before she could get the words out, my grandmother's hand, quick and efficient, slapped my mother's cheek. She was used to the sharp spark of my grandmother's touch, but the flame left smoldering on my mother's face still caught her off guard. My mother had assumed my grandmother would feel equally insulted by the prospect of participating in this kind of wedding ceremony, especially given it would be my grandmother's role to perform the ceremonial wedding bath, where she would be asked to pour a small vessel of flower-infused water over my mother's head to signify the bride's vow of purity and chastity. It was from my grandmother's daily lessons that my mother knew her place as Malay and Chinese. Why would she want my mother to do this just for some rich paperwhite? And my mother knew that, because of how wealthy my father was, their wedding would be splashed across all the papers. It would humiliate her to disrespect the Javanese people like this, such an ostentatious offense. She would lose face just as her groom would lift his own upwards for everyone to see. It made her want to gag.

"Daughter, I don't want to hear another word of this. You will marry this man however he wants. Do you know what I sacrifice for you, what he will give us, give my grandchildren? We have no means to be picky. You know how they are. They hold all the power. We just play the cards we are given. Understand?"

My grandmother's face was as stern as the sting that pulsated in my mother's skin. My mother nodded, holding back her tears. This is the moment it truly sank in for my mother all she was giving up to please this stranger who would soon be her husband and to appease my grandmother and build for herself a better life than the one she had inherited by virtue of her birth. It was starting to become clear to her the true price of monetary comfort. She felt a great sadness in her heart for the agency she would lose in this new life, the freedom to be herself gone. Sure, she had lived as a poor teenager. She and her mother worked themselves to the bone, but at least they could be pure of heart, sincere to themselves. None of that mattered anymore. What could she say? How could she give up the life this marriage promised, the material wealth and ease? She did not come from a country like America. She did not get to choose. And besides, she had been raised to obey her mother. It was clear that the decision simply was not up to her.

Although strong-willed and independent, my mother had still been raised a dutiful Southeast Asian girl, which meant you always submitted to the mandate of the mother. She knew she had no choice but to go along with this marriage, even though at this point, she was beginning to harbor an anxiety that was quickly shifting into despair over what the rest of her life would look like. My mother would take the back-crushing days of hard labor with her mother over this fancy, empty life any day. But that was no longer for her to say. Her mother had decreed it, and it was so. So, you see, it was not just an arranged marriage because of the tycoon. That she could have easily said no to. It was her mother's wishes she had to comply with the most. After all that her mother had done for her in her young life, it was the least she could give her in return.

If she had been in love with this man, the ceremony would have been a vision my mother could have only concocted in her dreams. The tycoon arranged for my mother's traditional wedding outfit to be specially designed and tailored to fit my mother's tapered form. My mother wore our traditional outfit, what we call a kebaya, but in white, so as to also offer a nod to my father's American tradition. My mother's hair, set in the traditional gelungan (a kind of formal bun), was protected by a long white veil embroidered with lace. Her face was cloaked in white powder with just a touch of rouge on each cheekbone, her lips stained scarlet. My father wore a special outfit in the same shade to match my mother appropriately, accompanied by a garland of white flowers resting around his neck.

My mother did not let her feelings be known during the wedding ceremony—although, when I was a teenager, about the age she was when she married my father, she admitted to me, as she told me the story of how she and my father met, that she wept during the entire traditional bathing ceremony, safe in the knowledge no one would see her tears as they merged with the water that masked her face. She washed her future husband's feet to symbolize her vow of devotion and subservience while they each offered each other three balls of rice formed with their hands. But mostly, my mother tried not to think about her impending future with my father; she spent the time musing on the life she had shared up to this point with her mother and the contentment it previously gave her, even when most of the days the two shared together consisted of physical labor that often broke the skin and strained the joints. My mother wondered if she would ever feel that happy again. As she and her new husband accepted the blessings from the tycoon's rich and unfamiliar guests, she tried to envision the life of her future child and hoped this sacrifice would give her child a better life than the one she imagined she was preparing to inhabit herself—bountiful, but without such sacrifice.

A few days later, my mother woke in her new bed, a far cry from where she once rested her head, with a new sleeping mate, my grandmother now in her own bed in a nearby room. Given my parents' life together had begun as a business proposition and given the significant age gap that already existed between them, the very idea of my mother consenting to the sexual union of my father's arduous desire wasn't exactly realistic. Even so many years later, after she has already passed on from this life, it's hard to talk about or even imagine her first night of sleep wedded to my father. I know it led to my birth—and still, it pains me to think that my arrival came from such torment. Yet, I know so many others who have suffered similar fates. Regardless, my mother woke in her new home determined to accept her new position as my father's object and the new life now bestowed on her as a gift. It was her only option as she saw it; otherwise, if she were to really consider what little power and agency she had for the rest of her days, she couldn't have possibly gone on.

In my earliest memories, my mother was quite enchanted with me, and I was equally enthralled with her and her loving nature. She had long ceased living the life of a practicing Muslim, but she often told the story of my childhood as though I were a blessing from Allah, proof this new life was worth what she had given up. My mother lavished me with endless affection, probably more than was healthy for my spirited personality. Even when I disobeyed her outright, she almost never scolded me, perhaps trying to compensate for my father's neglect and often foul and violent temper. In those early years, I found my mother's deep and abiding regard for me was more than enough for all I could ever need. There were times my father's menacing and biting tone—and at times, accompanying hand—could cause me to whimper or retreat into myself for several hours, or even days, after the incident had occurred and my father had long moved on with his day. But, for the most part, my mother doted on me in hopes that I would easily forget how quickly the smallest misstep from me could fill my father with such disdain and contempt. My mother's pleasure and happiness mattered far more to me than any pain my father could cause me. Limitless was the distance I would travel to keep her content, especially after one of my father's darker moods when he would use his hand to keep her in line. There was no doubt in my mind that keeping her happier than my father ever could, or desired, was my one true duty and responsibility. And I would stop at nothing to fulfill it.

For those first few years, I felt we were in it together—she was my dearest companion, my twin, my little ballerina twirling in front of her reflection in a velvet-lined music box. And I found no quandary with this as I was the same ballerina twirling for her amusement—we were both trinkets of pleasure. Life had been given by and through one another. It would take many, many years for me to examine this idea and watch the mechanism that had kept me afloat for so long swiftly fall apart.

It was somewhere between the ages of five and ten that my father would return home from a fateful business trip with a *gift* for my mother that would flip my beautiful little music-box world upside down. My father had traveled to Norway for a few days to conduct some business meetings. As he was taking a walk after a meeting that didn't turn out quite the way he'd hoped, my father happened upon a cherubic toddler playing outside on a square of grass in front of a small orphanage. The tot had curls that looked spun of gold with the same sparkling blue eyes my father recognized in his own reflection. Just as he had a few years prior upon meeting my mother, he envisioned no scenario in his mind that would prevent him from taking this child home. At long last, my father would finally possess a child untainted by my mother's dark skin and foreign blood, a child no one would question as his own, as happened often when we would go out for brunch or on the rare occasion my father would take me to the park without my mother in attendance. It seemed strange that this would bother him the way it did, as he was the one to choose my mother in a distant land to have as his wife and the mother of his child. But, as I'm sure you know just as well as I do, whiteness rears its head in ways that continue to stupefy the rest of us. Whatever the case, I was clearly my mother's child, my father rationalized, so it was only fair he, too, should have a child that held his complexion and likeness to reflect and adore him in the same measure.

As my father prepared for his trip home, he convinced himself, and me in turn, that this present was not for him or even my mother. He called my mother just before his plane took off and said mysteriously, "I have the most wondrous present for Zoelle. Tomorrow she shall have it."[21] At the time, I took his words with the utmost seriousness, that little Ezra, as he was introduced to me, was mine to nurture, cradle, and love. Like the Velveteen Rabbit I still carried around with me even after his eyes fell out of his head and his body was so loved up he had become ratted and worn. I felt little Ezra was so deeply part of me that every wound or affection directed his way was also happening directly to me. We called each other Cousin, but our link to one another extended so much farther than that of mere distant kin. All I knew was this: He was going to be

---

21 Shelley, *Frankenstein;*

mine forever.

李

As I listened to Dr. Frank's story, I couldn't help but think of Ma, of how even when I was too small to know better, all the love she poured over me like a thick syrup was not built to last. How sweet the syrup, but its thickness suffocated me until I couldn't breathe.

Even in those early years, before she left, Ma's love felt so deep and unbinding, but there was an edge to the love that felt impossible to sustain. What if she had loved me a little less, what if she had allowed herself to be a little more real? Just before the internship began, I visited a friend traveling through town with their partner and their two small children. We sat outside on a wooden bench, drinking ale and eating shrimp tacos, the juice dripping down our palms as we caught up. She was a friend from my time on the streets, and both of our lives had changed greatly since we had last seen one another. It had been many years since we had kept in touch, before she'd found her partner, before they'd given birth to their two small daughters. One of the daughters was in want of some attention, and she wedged her body between my friend's armpit and rib cage. She suctioned the air out like a piece of plastic plastered against a mirror, just like Ba and I did all those years ago, our sticky bodies tethered as we slumbered in the car in the middle of the afternoon in front of that dumpling house. It was a rare moment of joy between the two of us, and watching such a similarly tender scene as an adult made me smile to myself.

After a few minutes of holding her child next to her body while she continued her conversation, my friend said something to her child I didn't expect a mother to say.

"Can you go play with your sister?" she asked brusquely, a question phrased more as a dictate.

"It's boring. I don't want to," the child whined, nestling deeper into her side as a response, a sweet rebellion.

"Well, I'm going to finish this beer with my friend, and your hovering next to me is annoying me. I'd like you not to bother me until this beer is empty, please," my friend retorted.

The child rolled her eyes and promptly but begrudgingly detached her body from her mother's. And I was taken with how the child responded. She wasn't particularly insulted or even disappointed that her mother didn't want her company at this particular moment. It was an interaction between mother and child I'd never quite seen before. I often think of that moment, of the freedom a mother can have in taking herself off a pedestal, the same one that the child often mounts with her.

If Ma hadn't felt the pressure to love me so perfectly, or

even Ba for that matter, would she have stayed? She reached out to me through social media some years back. Ma said she'd been thinking about how she left, that she wanted to mend things. She asked if I was open to meeting with her. I replied that I would meet with her and gave her a few options for times that I was available. I asked her to meet me at a nearby park a few days later during my day off, a place that was neutral but relatively private. I agreed to meet with her mostly out of curiosity to hear what she would say, how she could possibly atone for how she left us. I would never find out what she had to say, if anything. She postponed three or four times before I told her I couldn't handle how difficult it seemed for her to make this one commitment to me, especially after having made so few in my life. At first, Ma tried to play the victim, but this was a mechanism I already knew from before. I wasn't interested in carrying that story for her, which is exactly what I told her. Our back-and-forth eventually sputtered out. I haven't heard from her since.

But now, hearing Dr. Frank's story of how much she and her mother idolized each other, I wonder if Ma just could never release the pressure she'd built into herself to be the perfect image of a mother. How much space did that image put between the two of us, between love and anger and disappointment and sadness and resentment and trust and safety? When a mother leads a child to also mother the mother, does the child cease to exist?

Z

Although at times my mother and father became territorial of the beings to which they felt they owed their every happiness—my mother of me and my father of little Ezra, who in his smallness was easier to adore—for the most part the two of us lived out our days endlessly attached to one another. My mother was required to cook for us as well as clean the enormous mansion my father provided us. My mother would cook simple Indonesian dishes for us during the week, like nasi goreng (a fried rice dish she made with a fried egg and whatever meat she could find at the market) or a curry with paratha and potatoes. Over the weekend, my grandmother would make us more lavish meals—ribs with sambal or saté with a rich peanut sauce. In the beginning, my father would relish in the foods my mother and grandmother would make, but he grew quickly tired of the heat in all the dishes, and so my mother would make a special American meal for him in addition to our own.

And certainly, as my father had always expected my mother to behave with deference and excessive gratitude to him for the life she now occupied and grateful for the child he made possible, I found caring for little Ezra much less anxiety-ridden and therefore more enjoyable than my mother did. In the first few months Ezra lived with us, I felt great shame at neglecting my mother who had been the center of my world thus far; but once I saw that our happiness together brought her great comfort, I settled into my role as little Ezra's guide, partner, sibling, cousin, and beloved.

Little Ezra, possibly from his years as an infant in the orphanage, had a more delicate and tenderhearted disposition. I believe it was for this reason my father grew increasingly disinterested in the little trinket he decided to pick up one day. Ezra often sought my father's approval, but to no avail. Since he was the only son, my father did not discipline him with a harsh tongue and hand the way he did my mother and me, but even so, his neglect of Ezra caused Ezra's sensitivity to have a kind of edge I found frightening at times. I would learn that I had much to fear of the storm that my adoration mixed with my father's ice-cold distance would provoke.

Ezra was a darling child, however, and I loved holding him in my lap and twisting his Shirley Temple curlicues around my fingers while he nestled up against my chest and fell asleep. As he grew into a young boy, he was fond of fingering the many sarongs that our mother fastidiously hung in my parents' walk-in closet, and I always imagined he would end up a tailor or even a clothing designer. I'm sure this was one of the reasons my father had no interest in bonding further with Ezra—my father was, as I'm sure it's clear, what some would call a man's man, and would often insist that my mother scold Ezra so that he would understand the codes of masculinity he needed to follow. My mother humored my father but didn't have the heart to do this, so she would often ask me to dissuade him from the finer arts of textiles and design. Although I loved to shower my little Ezra with affection and tenderness, I was too fixated on my own intellectual pursuits to include him or keep him from his own desires. I grew more inquisitive of how machines were built and the minds responsible for the mechanisms behind their power. While Ezra took stencil to paper to design various floral patterns to adorn one of our mother's new sarongs she would have custom-made by my father's resident tailor—it was assumed by the three of us that my father was to never hear of it—I was preoccupied with dismantling my toys and discerning how to reassemble them. The universe was a problem I was desperate to decipher.

I had no interest in indoctrinating Ezra with whatever codes my father believed a man ought to obey. As far as I was concerned, it was this ideology that had kept my father himself from being a kind and loving parent and spouse. From as far back as I could remember, I knew what I was, I knew that the bodies I was drawn to most were the ones that looked and felt like mine, but that internally I felt more male than female, more he than she. How could I change what was most inherent in Ezra when I wasn't even willing to do it to myself?

A few years after my father ushered Ezra into our lives,

perhaps when he realized he would never have the son he always imagined, my mother convinced him to purchase a modest ranch house in a small desert town in West Texas. By that point, it was becoming increasingly difficult to keep my father's rages to a minimum, and as I look back on that time, it's my suspicion my mother urged him to buy the country house in case she would eventually be forced to leave him.

We got used to blocking out the heated arguments that would take place between our parents at all hours of the night. When I was very young, before I learned to speak and when I had just learned to walk, I remember waking up in the middle of the night to my mother's cries. In the hallway, I saw my father with his arm awkwardly around my mother's shoulder, a haphazard attempt at consoling her as she dried her eyes with the sleeve of her silk robe, her whimpers devastating, even to my infant self. One side of her face was red, and although I did not immediately pick up on the fact that it was because my father had begun to strike her when their arguments became heated, I could feel the violence and secrecy of their troubles. It frightened me, but I knew, even as a small child, not to broach the subject with my mother.

I wanted very much to shield my new cousin, sibling, and plaything from the terrifying dynamics of our caregivers, but the tension between my parents only worsened as I got older. When little Ezra was very small, he would run to me during the times my father started in on my mother—when he couldn't find the remote control or on a rare occasion when my mother would mouth off to him in response to his many provocations.

I would hold Ezra in my lap and I would coil my finger around his golden curls, the one thing that always calmed him. The longer I spooled my finger around his little ringlets, the quieter his cries would become, until he would ultimately fall asleep. There was something in the control it gave me to soothe my little Ezra in this way that was a comfort to me as well. Like a little girl brushing the hair of her favorite porcelain doll long after her hair had become untangled.

As for me, regardless of the many times I saw my mother submit to my father or the number of times I dried her tears, I had completely convinced myself my mother was superhuman and could handle anything my father would throw her way, even when there was much evidence to the contrary. I still remember the way my body would flinch upon hearing a glass shatter or the intolerable smack of my father's hand on my mother's supple skin, but it was, to put it simply, easier for me to deny the gravity of my father's anger and how it possibly impacted my mother than to contend with how helpless I felt regarding my mother's unhappiness. I think perhaps even my obsession with Ezra was my way of avoiding how little I could do to keep my father from destroying my mother, day by day, strike by strike. My inability to save my mother got redirected onto little Ezra, and this distracted me from seeing the bruises on her arms or the darkened exhaustion in her eyes, her dulled skin. The fact that I couldn't keep my father from taking out his small quibbles and large rages on my most beloved reflection was too much to bear. Even though I saw her as superhuman, I never saw her as someone that could rescue me from my father. However, he was more interested in keeping her in line than even Ezra or me.

When my grandmother wasn't out shopping or cooking the big weekend meals, she mostly kept to herself in her own room. She almost never intervened, which somehow I never thought to question. There were days where she would take a car into town to get her nails done or refresh the coloring of her hair when the gray would start to show again, and she would come home showering the two of us with beautiful gifts, but other than that, we didn't have much of a relationship with her. My mother never taught us Indonesian or Malay or even Mandarin, and my grandmother spoke almost no English. The language barrier made communication awkward. My father forbade my mother to teach us any words from her birth languages. I always wondered, once I knew the story of how my grandmother insisted that my mother go through with the wedding to my father, how my mother felt about her own mother's inability to protect her as she witnessed my father abuse her while living in the same house. Sometimes, when my father was out of town, I would hear my mother crying in my grandmother's room, but my grandmother would immediately silence her with a few sharp words I couldn't understand. On days like those, I would hear my mother slam the door to my grandmother's room and return to the one she shared with my father. She would not emerge for several hours.

Soon enough, the three of us began to spend all of our summers at the country house, and this helped a great deal because my father often had to stay at our house in the city in order to take care of business obligations. It wasn't long until it was a given that my father would not even pretend to make the effort to join us for long stretches, which led to some years of truly joyous memories for the four of us, including our grandmother. But even during those summers when my mother thought we could take a short trip here or there to Indonesia without him catching on, he would always find ways to show up unplanned. I always felt he just wanted to make things difficult for my mother, and thus, for the rest of us. He felt omnipresent and ever-distant all at once.

But, for the most part, he was refreshingly absent. To be honest, I think he enjoyed the solitude just as much as we enjoyed being free of his unbearable temperament. And I'm sure, now that I'm thinking about it, that he must have had a mistress, or maybe more, back in the city (or maybe in a place not connected to either of our homes) where he spent the many hours. I assume she held the same shade of his fair white skin, his softened, pink, tulip-shaped lips, those doe-eyed, blue sparkling marbles that my mother saw as so inimitable, but now that she lived in America, realized were no anomaly.

As much as I'm ashamed to admit this, I grew tired of watching my mother disappear at my father's hand. But I had no right to judge as I had no ability to stop him myself the few times that he would strike me or when he would take out whatever grievance he was experiencing in his professional life on my mother over chipped toenail polish or a spot she hadn't yet cleaned on the marble countertops. If he came home in a mood and she didn't instantly come to fulfill his every need and wish, he would immediately lash out at her.

There is one occasion I remember, although I'm sure there were more, when my mother reached her limit. It was on a Saturday afternoon after we'd had a delightful day with her. She had taken us out for crepes at a food truck in the center of town. The day, filled with laughter and joy, was a particularly beautiful one. The sun was bright in the sky, but not too intense, and a breeze kissed our shoulders as we ate our after-lunch gelato, a splurge my mother indulged in only when she was in an especially fine mood. She had taken some unusual time away from cooking and cleaning to spend the day with us, and asked after what I was reading lately and what Ezra had seen lately that had inspired him. The day felt magical and new.

When we got back to the house, we were all surprised to find my father had been waiting on us, clearly enraged to not find us exactly where he wanted us. I could feel my mother's body tense and tighten next to me, as though getting ready for battle. Which, I suppose, she was.

"Darlings, go to your rooms. I'll handle this," she said, her mood turning from sunflower yellow to thunder, just like that.

I couldn't hear everything, although Ezra and I pressed our ears next to each other against my bedroom door.

"How dare you leave the house without telling me? Do you have no appreciation for what I've given you? It is so obvious to me that you care for those kids more than you have ever cared for me."

"They certainly treat me better than you do," my mother

muttered under her breath, words we could barely make out.

"Excuse me? What did you say?" My father didn't care, ever, to keep his voice down.

"If you hate us so much, why are you here? If I knew I would only stay a servant to your every whim and mood, I would have preferred to be poor in Jakarta with my mother, where at least I could count on her love. Even that you have destroyed. Nothing is safe around you," she said.

Then we heard a crash.

Ezra and I peeled ourselves off the door and ran to my mother, curled up in the fetal position on the living room floor, blood and snot and tears running across the hardwood. From that moment onward, I understood why she remained so silent. But I never truly understood why she wouldn't leave him. I was too afraid to ask.

*

Ezra and I filled out the days with our own adventures after my mother would drop us off in the middle of the town square. Ezra would meander through the main thoroughfares, snapping photos of locals with the vintage film camera my mother had found for him in the flea market, or stroll through the art museum's most recent installations, whereas I would hole myself up in the one independent used bookstore in town with one subject of inquiry or another for hours on end with the few dollars my mother could spare from the allowance my father gave her, using so little of it he wouldn't notice.

I was quite self-satisfied with my own sources of knowledge and because of this I found that companions other than Ezra were of little use to me. Even Ezra was not someone with whom I shared my curiosities, but more like a doll or an imaginary friend I adored in whatever way fit my fancy. I had no interest in the other teenagers my age that also visited the town during the summers like we did. They were rich like we were, but white and disinterested in the finer pursuits of life. We didn't really share much in common with them. I was perfectly happy to scour the bookstore's contents for the answers to whatever question I was determined to solve at the time. If what I found wasn't sufficient, I would walk the block and a half over to the library to find more tomes I hoped would appease my endless curiosity. I was perfectly at home spending the long hours of each day cradled in my own solitude and never felt a need or want for any human to accompany me, or for any social interaction, for that matter.

That is, until I met her. Hana.

Given that the town where we summered was so white-populated, Hana immediately stood out to me as I could tell just by looking at her that she was a hybrid, just like me. Her skin was dark, like my mother and grandmother, and her copper curls glinted when light struck them, reminding me fondly of the way sunlight hit the orange seashells I collected at the beach when I was young. I kept them in an old milk bottle I had found at the thrift store in the town square, and my mother would often pick out her favorite when Ezra and I were away from the house for the day. When we returned home, I would often find her rubbing it back and forth in her hand to comfort her. Sometimes, if she was in a particularly good mood, she would tell me stories about the Pink Beach just off the coast of Indonesia and show me a shell or two that she took from one of the wealthy homeowners she cleaned for. "The wealthy have so many things, they don't miss one or two," she would say with a wink. But most of the time, if I found her rubbing one of the orange shells from my milk bottle, it was a clue something was on her mind.

Hana's eyes were round but tapered at the edges, like mine, and she also had freckles that spotted the bridge of her nose and cheeks, just like I did. I found it was both her uniqueness and the traits we shared that drew me to her, although we were not identical. The whiteness of Hana's teeth popped out against her skin in a way I found mesmerizing, like pearls rising to the shore. The minute I saw her, I was captivated and would stop at nothing to become close to her.

The first time I happened upon Hana, she was walking down a street in the town square during an unusually busy afternoon. I tried to casually follow her but I eventually lost her in the crowd. The pull I felt towards her was so strong that, even though I knew Ezra was waiting for me so that we could take the bus back home, I couldn't stop until I found her again.

It didn't take long.

I saw her again in the other small independent bookstore in town, not the used one but the one that carried the latest bestsellers, and even though I was out of breath from my extensive search for this mystery person, I opened the glass door to the bookstore as casually as I could muster, whistling the breath out of my body as slow as possible until my heart rate matched that of the other customers. As the bells attached to the door jingled, announcing my entrance, I saw my mystery girl take a curious look over her shoulder at me. She wore loose-fitting mustard trousers, fine dark leather sandals, and a magenta crop top made of silk. A satin blue ribbon was woven through one of her ginger spirals. She was the most elegant and striking person I had ever laid my eyes on. Not altogether unlike the moment Ezra first entered my life, I felt this person was for me and me alone. But, she was not given to me as a gift to adore like little Ezra, and so I hoped it wouldn't take too much convincing to become close to her.

To my shock and delight, it was Hana that found her way over to me as I pretended to peruse the philosophy section, her arm grazing mine as she grabbed a book in front of me. As I stepped back to give her room, she introduced herself.

"Hi, how are you? My name is Hana. Do you want to have a boba at that tea house down the street?" Her smile was gradual and luscious, like honey coating the skin. That's when I realized not everyone was as easy to control as little Ezra. It was disorienting to be in the passenger seat with Hana, but at the same time, it was also exhilarating and unpredictable. I was taken with her from that first meeting over milk tea and tapioca, and over the time we shared, it was a constant struggle to stay ever-present to my work as thoughts of Hana would constantly disrupt my focus. Of course, she wasn't to blame, and I still feel deeply remorseful of how our relationship inevitably came to an end.

Hana and I immediately formed a bond, the likes of which I had never before experienced with anyone. It was far more complex than the charming attachment even Ezra and I had with one another.

As Hana and I got to know each other, I learned that her father was Japanese and her mother was from Virginia, and so we spent many hours commiserating on what it was like to have within us such differing, warring worlds. Her father was a simple furniture salesman, and her mother waitressed in a diner down the street from the bookstore. At times, she would sing at jazz clubs in the larger cities that were close by. I knew the minute that Hana told me that her mother was a waitress which restaurant she worked at, as her similarly untamed curls and striking beauty were hard to miss. I giggled when I told her this, and hid my face in my hand to hide my blushing skin. That's when Hana knew that when I told her I remembered her mother's beauty, I meant it to reveal what I thought of her as well.

I had never told another girl I was drawn to her or even admitted that I was attracted more to girls than to boys. I wouldn't exactly say that I consciously made my attraction known to Hana, either. It was as though the impulse to reveal my innermost feelings for Hana came from within my body, but also beyond it, and I didn't think about the ramifications before I told her what she meant to me. It took time for Hana to respond with her feelings in kind. I knew she felt somewhat the same for me by her acceptance of my attractions towards her, for not withdrawing from me when it was clear I meant to court her.

I would later learn she had surprisingly accepting parents who were also her greatest confidantes. They had guided her well and taught her not to rush into new relationships. I would later become resentful that Hana had the kind of parents a young queer person would dream of, not only because she could rely on them for support, but also because it was wanting to stay close to them that ultimately kept her farther from me.

I didn't know what kind of a romantic partner I was, for there was never anyone I fell for who would have brought those aspects of my character out of me. When I became attracted to girls I passed by in the square on my way to the bookstore or the library, I never allowed myself to indulge in the feelings, which faded away quickly. When I met Hana, I had been waist-high in my intellectual pursuits, and romantic encounters, or love, were the last thing on my mind. Nothing tended to conquer my passion for my studies. As Hana and I became closer, I was surprised to find lurking within me the predilections and impulses of a gentleman. It was not only the manner I desired to pursue Hana that felt most gentlemanly; it was also how I wanted to dress myself for the occasions I would take Hana out on the town and other patterns of behavior inspired by my favorite Elizabethan novels and films that felt gentlemanly.

Over the course of our relationship, we would spend time having dinner with Hana's parents, which brought up for me a myriad of complicated feelings. Hana's parents had a sweetness with each other I wanted desperately to witness between my own parents. All I had seen my parents express was anger and fear. Still, it was deeply affirming to have Hana's parents seem truly happy for us, to share our love with any other people besides the two of us. Her parents were a true partnership, even all the way down to the dinner table. We would have ramen and homemade sushi next to collard greens and chicken fried steak. It was impossible to resist their charms. Ever so often, Hana's father would touch his hand to the small of her mother's back or beam at her with just a look, and it was enough to bring me to tears.

Shortly after we met, I planned to borrow the family car and drive Hana to a nearby city, where they were staging a queer adaptation of *Romeo & Juliet.* We had made a plan that we would dress for the occasion, even if we were the only ones to do so. We were young queers in love. In order to fully take on the fantasy I was eager to lavish on Hana, I needed money not made readily available to me. It required confiding in someone. My grandmother was too conventional and would never understand. I tried my mother and hoped for the best, for I knew if I misjudged her ability to accept me, it could have disastrous consequences.

On one of our outings into town, I sat in the car with my mother while we waited for Ezra to finish perusing his favorite gallery's latest exhibition.

"Ma?" I started, unsure of how to begin.

"Mm." My mother looked out the window aimlessly. It was only after she heard me clear my throat she realized this was no ordinary conversation.

"What is it? Is it Ezra? Did Pa do something?" My mother's line of questions made me feel worse for bringing this up, for wanting dapper outfits and my mother's support of a brand new romance, which might not even go anywhere, when there were far graver concerns to consider in our lives. But my heart needed her approval.

"No, no, nothing like that, Ma. Remember that new friend I told you about? Hana?" My mother exhaled and started looking out the window again.

"Oh, yes. Her father Japanese, right? Mother is pretty, works in restaurants and sings out of town?" I blushed, thinking of Hana again.

"Yes, that's her. Well, um. But. I, um, I am taking her out next week, to see a play. A date. And I want to dress like a calalai."

My mother said nothing at first, just raised her eyebrow, darkened and shaped with black kohl.

"Date? A calalai? Really? How did you learn this? You know this doesn't come from our region, right?" The anxiety of the moment overwhelmed me.

"Yes, I know. In a book I found at the bookstore. But, that's the easiest way to explain how I feel," I said sheepishly. *Calalai* was a term I read in a book I found on the Bugis, the largest ethnic group in South Sulawesi, Indonesia. Their language accounts for five different gender categories, and *calalai* is their gender term for masculine women. The first time I read the passage in the book, my skin tingled in recognition and validation of a way my body felt that I'd never heard or even knew existed. And even better, it was a word that came from the same country as my own mother, as close to my birthright as I could get.

"You are dressing for fun, like costume, or you really feel you're calalai?" She peered into my eyes, which I kept downward. I didn't know how to answer her, so I started to cry, holding my head in my hands. My mother had never been one for my tears. I imagine the same for your father. She awkwardly patted my shoulder, then roughly grabbed my chin with one hand and demanded it upwards to look back at her.

"Okay, Zo. Okay. You must be very careful, because you do not know with these Texans. Even in parts of Indonesia, even when we have words for, you know, people that are different. It is still not easy. And there is your father to worry about. Be careful, okay? And, you must never call yourself calalai publicly, especially to Indonesians. It is not our language to claim. Okay?" I nodded.

"But where is this play?" Once my mother started talking logistics, I knew it would be okay.

"It is not here. It is far away."

"Okay, do you need money? For outfit?" I nodded again, wiping the tears from my face now that I saw Ezra walking towards our car.

"Zoelle, listen." She stroked my hair, then, an impulse that was infrequent but of a comfort to me.

"Do not tell Ezra about this. Do not tell your father. And be very careful how you are with her, or any girl, in public. This is for your own good, understand? The world can be hard. It is too harsh already to us. Oh, and your grandmother, your nenek. She will never understand. I will hide some money for outfit in your pillowcase."

She paused for a beat, thinking. "I think she is nice girl," she said slowly, and the smallest smile inched across her mouth.

I grinned as warmth radiated through my chest. Just a moment later, I saw Ezra walking towards the car, and so I tried to look as casual as possible. And so it was that I learned I was a calalai and to keep it secret.

I picked Hana up in our family car the day of the play, wearing a deep purple waistcoat, a pink ruffled blouse with a high neck, and forest-green men's trousers I had my father's tailor alter for my shape. I went to the barber shop on the way. It was a Thursday night, a day I knew the one woman barber worked, and I asked her to give me a men's cut with a tight fade. I can't articulate how it felt to come into my own body, my own style, my own calalai. She knew that I was about to head to my first date, and so she sprinkled talcum powder against my neck and as she brushed it against my skin, I sighed with pleasure at my new self. And with my mother's blessing. I only hoped Hana would approve.

Hana looked ravishing. Her red hair shone in a way it hadn't before. She wore an ankle-length, blue pleated skirt, a green satin button-down blouse, and soft pink ballet flats made to look like pointe shoes with a box toe and thick straps across the front. Her lips were painted a sparkling mauve, and her jade drop earrings shone against the rapidly dissolving daylight. As usual, she took my breath away, but it was deeply reassuring to see her react to my transformation. Impulsively, Hana took one hand and rubbed it against the back of my neck. I sighed audibly as Hana beamed at me, a smile I'd never seen before, as though she were seeing me for the first time.

I guess we both were.

*

Hana taught me about the Black and Asian scholars and thinkers who had a different angle than I would have formed myself on the subjects that fascinated me and shared with me the activists and philosophers that inspired her to further pursue social justice. I wasn't accustomed to sharing my ideas with another—even when we were closer, not even Ezra was privy to my deepest thoughts and investigations—but when I was with Hana, I felt cast under a spell, as though I was surprised by my own actions. Hana knew how to open me up, at least more than I would ordinarily, and before long, we were writing treatments for documentary shorts and abstracts for collaborative papers we might write one day for a conference or symposium we daydreamed about traveling to together. No one but my mother knew about Hana, and I kept it that way. Not only did I want her all to myself, but I feared even telling Ezra could expose us to my father. I didn't want to think about what that would mean. If Hana lived back in the city or my father were with us more in the little town in the country, it is possible I would have never gained the nerve to approach her, as I would have been terrified of how my father would have taken her gender or her darker skin (even though it matched that of my mother's) were he to come upon the two of us together.

As it was, Hana made me feel like I could do anything, and the more time we spent together, the more I could see the way I presented myself changing. Not only was I trying to seem more traditional back home, but I also began dressing one way in front of my family and another saved just for Hana, which I felt matched the true me.

I kept this double life a secret, even from my mother, until one day I was so caught up in our new love I forgot to change back into the clothes I had worn leaving the house, and my mother caught me carrying my father's briefcase that I had snuck out of the house that morning, dressed in a collared shirt, a paisley necktie, my father's leather oxfords (much too large for me but wearable), and a black trench.

Still floating on the clouds meant for only Hana, I couldn't even shut the front door before my mother had pulled me with extreme force into the laundry room by my wrist.

"Ma!" I cried out in pain, freeing my hand, and rubbing my wrist with the thumb of the opposing hand.

"Zoelle, what is this, ah?!" She pulled at my tie and lightly kicked the toe of my father's oxfords.

I bowed my head in shame, shocked out of my Hana reverie. There was nothing I could say. She knew.

"I just," I started meekly, my voice dropping. But she had no patience for me to bumble through my words. She grabbed my father's brown leather suitcase with the glinting gold locks from my hand.

"I told you. If he find out what you are, I cannot protect you!" she scream-whispered and started to cry. Her tears brought me out of whatever it was I was feeling at her abrasiveness. I held her in my arms, something I often did when I was younger, but she pulled away from me.

"No. Do not comfort me. Just be better. You already cut your hair after I told you not to let your father see. If you want to play at being a boy, it doesn't matter to me. But if he catch you, there will be nothing I can do! You know how he is. He is like bulldog. I wish it were different. But this is what we have. Okay? Go take off clothes and put back briefcase. And don't take your father's things again! It is not worth risk." She turned on her heel and left me in the laundry room in the dark.

My mother was not the type of mother to talk to about this. But my masculinity was not role-play or theater. I changed into an outfit that looked more like a tomboy than a grown man, but one my father would approve of, and snuck out to see Hana.

"Oh, Z," she said sympathetically after I told her what had happened. She held my head in her lap and stroked my short hair as I wept until out of breath.

*

It's shameful, after how intolerable it was to watch my father wield his rage as a weapon to force my mother (and, at times, me) to submit to his every want and need, to admit my father had instilled in me a ferocious temper, to realize how easily I could become unglued when Hana and I debated over what we remembered of a particular scholar and I would discover that I was wrong. I had a pathological need to be right that petrified me on the rare occasions I was able to acknowledge this demon inside me, but for the most part, Hana could settle my nerves in a way no one else had previously, so the tempers remained short-lived.

For the most part, I wasn't able to admit some of the darker truths behind my expressions of anger—that the further I traveled in my identity and ownership of being a calalai, I was inevitably taking on the only masculine model I had ever known: My abusive, violent, intolerably narcissistic father. Of course, there was Ezra, but he was more of a calabai (feminine man) than a traditional man, and therefore did not have the traits I imagined I would embody for myself.

I still remember the first time my rage flew most pointedly out of my body and landed on Hana as a target. It's almost too unbearable to speak of, even now, so many years later, but it's an important part of where our story ends up and what wretched end Hana met due to my own recklessness and vanity.

I was incredibly territorial about the work I intended to pursue, and I had just begun investigating the possibility of using stem cells to create an embryo without the need of sperm. As I began to fall deeper and deeper in love with Hana, the prospect of not needing a man's sperm to start a family of my own with Hana in the future was incredibly exciting to me. I was caught between male and female, man and woman, so it gave me great sadness and feelings of inadequacy to imagine I would need a man to create a child. It was actually Hana herself who first brought it to my attention that, based on the research available at the time, it was quite possible not to need an egg either.

We had decided this one day at the park, a common meeting place for us to hide from Ezra or others in town who might know my father, underneath a tree far away from where most congregated, where we could kiss and speak passionately about our favorite subjects without distraction or interruption, or uncomfortable gazes.

Hana sat down with a feverish acceleration, her breath coming out in short, heightened bursts, an infectious grin brightening her face. Just as she was about to tell me something I could see held for her a great deal of urgency, I took her face in both of my hands and kissed her for several minutes.

"I love when I see that passionate look on your face," I said to her as I came up for air, taking a hand and running it down her cheek. She smiled at me as she caught her breath, taking her own hand and touching the back of mine, which still rested on her face.

"Oh, I've been dying to see you. I'm always dying to see you," she said coquettishly. But I could tell there was more to her words of affection than just romance.

"What's going on? Did you find a new writer for us to dig into?" I asked casually, but I could tell it was far more important than one of our usual intellectual finds.

"Oh, no. It's so much better." As the words rushed out of her, she hefted her bag onto her lap and began to rummage through its contents. Something about the mystery surrounding what she had brought to our tryst sparked a bit of anxiety within me, but I couldn't quite place the reason behind it.

With her exquisite, delicate fingers, Hana laid out onto the blanket that held our snacks and books a number of articles on the latest innovations in stem cell research. One article in particular caught my eye. It focused on an experiment in which a live fetus was created without using sperm *or* egg. I could feel my adrenaline quicken within my skin but for an altogether different reason than for Hana.

"Handsome, look! We may not even need to use sperm or egg at all—" she started, excitedly. She began to point at the articles in her hand.

Without a moment's hesitation, I grabbed the articles from her and shred them to pieces with my bare hands. The little pieces of the work Hana reached for caught a breeze above our heads and flew into the air. Hana did not have time to react because the fury I unleashed startled her into silence, her mouth open in horror and confusion.

"How dare you do this! What made you think that my work—MY work—was for you to uncover? If you ever do anything like this again, you will be nothing to me. I will not speak to you, I will not see you, I will not so much as think your name ever, ever again. Do you understand me?"

My entire body trembled with the offense of what I considered her thievery of my future ambitions, work I had been solely focused on my entire life, years before I ever knew of Hana's existence. Before I could consider what it was I had done, Hana, with a kind of frightening composure, snatched all of her things in haste. You wouldn't even know she was upset save for the tears on the tender, smooth cheeks I had only moments before caressed with tenderness and love. She was ready to run from me. Although I hadn't yet come down from my fever, I tried to clutch her hand as she stumbled to her feet, knowing that once she left, I might never have the chance to do so again, but she yanked her hand away and left me on our blanket, alone.

After my breathing slowed, I stopped to consider what I had done. I went looking for her to repair the damage I had caused by my impulsive nature. I found her at the site of one of our first dates, a park bench underneath an expansive willow tree in the cemetery just on the outskirts of town. We often sat at that park bench and reflected to ourselves while holding one another's hand. I felt a tightness in my chest, a kind of guilt I couldn't possibly articulate the sensation of, but I knew I had no other choice but to push through to keep her with me, to have her mine for always.

"Darling. I don't even know what to say. It makes me absolutely sick to my stomach that my father's disgusting temper lives in me like this," I started. Hana held her face and torso away from me.

"I don't even know what came over me. You know this isn't me, don't you? What a gift you are. And look how I repaid my gratitude, to treat you like you were nothing more than an animal, or my servant. I am so sorry I took your generosity and ruined it." I curled my chest over my knees and hid my face in my hands.

"No, no, no, love," Hana implored, immediately rushing to drape me in her sweet touch. She sighed.

"I understand, my precious Z. I know you've been inside your work so intimately, in such isolation, for so many years. I should have handled it more delicately. I was just so excited to show you how you were clearly pursuing an innovation that could be possible for you and could make things so much easier for us in the future," Hana consoled me, gazing at me sympathetically while stroking my back. But, she didn't understand. I didn't want to follow the trends of the day, nor did I need her or anyone else to educate me on the strength of my ideas or future progress. I wanted to be the one to create them. I knew that I would. It was impossible to explain without displaying an untoward amount of hubris, and so, instead of arguing with her, I just accepted her touch and her laboring after me, and let her curls fall over me like a waterfall.

My episodes of rage didn't happen often, but that incident would not be the last time I would lose my temper on those I held most dear to me. When I indulged the thought, it would burn me to think of the possibility that my father's rage lived inside my blood, ready to be unleashed on any unwilling victim when I least suspected it. I could no longer simply see my father as a wretched beast and I his victim, for I was also a demon victimizing Hana just like my father had my mother. I consoled myself with the grim knowledge that at least it wasn't in my nature to strike Hana with my own hand. I couldn't imagine causing her physical harm, but I honestly wanted no aspect of his disposition to occupy any part of my temperament or personality. Little did I know I would cause her the most harm. But it is not time yet for that part of the story.

Summer especially was my chance not to consider my father at all, except when he suddenly stayed home for a while during his sporadic surprise visits, so I didn't give those tempers much mind in Hana's company. But that meant Hana and I developed a problematic pattern in which I lashed out at her whenever my possessive nature—either towards her or my work—was provoked, and she labored after me in efforts to calm me from my fits of rage. What was worse was that I made no effort to stop her. This wasn't all that different, I suppose, from what my own parents negotiated with one another, except my father had no interest in redemption, for he never saw himself as culpable. And because Hana seemed to have endless patience and energy to care for me in my moods, even when she was the target, I never considered behaving any differently. At the time, I felt that my recognition of what was most heinous in me was enough. I never stopped to consider how I expected Hana to stop at nothing to make me whole again—to stop me from my basest impulses and to save me from my own violent tongue. Changing my behavior wasn't something I ever considered possible, or necessary. Now, as I tell this story, I am painfully aware of how little I supported her own dreams, her own rages, her own griefs.

Meanwhile, little Ezra remained my sweet clementine to fawn over, like the beautiful fabrics he stroked as if they were the striped furs of a newborn kitten. Although I never shared my deepest desires with him, I expected him to always share all of his pleasures and joys with me (as well as our mother), and it never occurred to me to question the role I believed he held in both our lives. Not only that, but I expected it to remain the same always, for the duration of our lives together.

*

At first, I tried to blame the changes whirring within me—less like the potions of my studies, elixirs of life and potentiality, and more like a poison boiling in the blood—on the tiny town I was relegated to for most of my youth. I did not have friends or any other person to speak to about what mattered to me other than Hana, and at times, Ezra. I blamed this on the provincial and conservative Southerners that surrounded me, that even the other queers in the town were white and couldn't possibly understand what my life was like. My mind and my ambitions were outgrowing the limited resources of the small library and bookstore in town, and as my inquisitive nature grew more demanding and urgent, I found myself looking at everyone and every other factor outside of myself as the culprit for my short temper and possessive nature, my inability to listen to others' insights, to see what they could offer my path towards creating life. But it was when I shunned Ezra, my darling little wonder, that everything began to turn, like a fruit's softness turns from the ripeness of pleasure to the spoils of spores and disease. But it wasn't I who shunned Ezra first. As always, it started with my father. I was out with Hana when the worst of it happened.

When I returned home, I found my father's car parked

in front of the street to our house—an unexpected and early return, but one he was starting to do more often the older we both became. It was as though he explicitly would return at random times in order to catch one of us in behavior unsuitable to his liking, as though he explicitly returned home to work out whatever frustrations that day brought him on our skin or the container of our home, which was tranquil and sweet in his absence.

I could feel my heart quicken in its tempo within my chest, my hands quaking in my pockets, as they always did when he was home. I usually took my time walking the long walkway that split our palatial front garden filled with my grandmother's favorite plants from Indonesia; luckily Texas's climate was humid enough to provide them what they needed to flourish. On each half of the front yard, just in front of my grandmother's flowerbeds, stood two grand oak trees. Usually, on a day when I knew my father was waiting inside, I spent some time staring up at the trees that shielded my eyes from direct contact with the sunlight. But on this particular day, Ezra's screams stopped me from my meditation. He had whimpered in my arms every time my parents fought, but I had never heard him shriek like that before. I could hear him audibly from the lawn where I knelt to pick up the delicate bloom of a blue hydrangea that had fallen from the bush. I dropped it onto the ground and ran into the house.

My father stood in the middle of the living room with a tin pail. He wore an oxford shirt with the sleeves rolled up past his elbows, exposing his tan, muscular arms. His hair was unusually unkempt, sweaty and plastered to his forehead. Next to the pail on the floor, in a haphazard lump, sat all of Ezra's beautiful silks and the sarongs he had painted and embroidered for my mother. She was screaming from inside my parents' bedroom to be let out; my father had locked her inside. My grandmother, as usual, was in her room, silent. I wondered how she could stay in her room when sweet little Ezra sat next to the lump of his favorite possessions, in the fetal position, imploring my father to stop.

"I never meant to disappoint you," Ezra blubbered through his tears, sitting up now, his knees pressed against his chest, rocking himself back and forth like a child.

It was as though my father didn't hear him. He gingerly took each piece of fabric and calmly placed it in the pail. No words. Just that repetitive action, again and again.

I stood behind the two of them, frozen in my body, afraid of what would happen next. I couldn't move. I couldn't speak. I could only watch in horrified silence.

"Your mother could never give me a son of my own. We had your sister. Although she is beautiful and has a brilliant mind, she is cursed with your mother's dark skin. When I found you playing in the grass, I knew you would be the one I would raise in my shadow, to extend the family line, to provide for your mother and your grandmother long after I'm gone. But, I don't know what happened. No matter what I do, your mother taints everything she touches. I will not have this. If I find you have returned to this useless feminine pursuit against my orders, given all I have provided for you, I will not think twice about returning you to the orphanage. If they will even have you. The old ones cost the most resources and are the hardest to adopt. You know this better than me. I will not bear the burden of responsibility if you end up on the street. We will not speak of this again."

By this time, each and every item that was Ezra's whole world filled the pail to the very top. Ezra's words were incomprehensible through his tears. He reached for a handful of my father's jeans at his ankles, but my father kicked Ezra away with his steel-toed boot. Then my father took a box of matches from his pocket, struck a single match, and set the pail's contents on fire.

It is impossible to describe what happened to my darling cousin and brother then.

As the sarongs lit up in orange flames and turned black as death, the pitch of Ezra's voice rose up and out of his body like a wounded animal—the light in his eyes that I so dearly cherished snuffed out.

What is there to say about how a father can break a boy-child? He was never the same after that. In some ways, in a striking turn of events, my gender and my detestable brown skin shielded me from my father's demands. I was not his wife. I was not his son. He wanted nothing to do with me. What that meant was that he placed no expectation on what I was to become. Because sperm did not live inside me, because I was not a member of the chosen sex, I would never be expected to further the family line—even though Ezra shared none of my father's biological or genetic makeup. I became untouchable. But now that I think about it, it was this inadvertent armor I wore that perhaps contributed to turning me into the monster that I would become.

After that fateful day between Ezra and my father, little Ezra, as I knew him, was dead. Never to return. Even before then, I had become so fixated on my own work, on Hana, that I no longer had time for Ezra or even my mother. I was intolerable in those days, and when I wasn't sneaking around with Hana during the days my father was back in the city, I was at home with my nose in books, keeping to myself, and plotting my eventual escape. But no longer were the days when Ezra would sit on my lap while I stroked his curls as he slept open-mouthed on my chest. The day after the fire, Ezra asked my mother to take him into the city to the barbershop in the town square and had his curls cut off.

He began to accompany my father on his business trips during the summers. It was unclear to me if he was eager to learn the trade of my father's family or if he was performing adulation for my father, hoping it would appease him and quiet his boiling rage. Of course, my father ate it up as though it were one of my mother's custards. It made me sick to my stomach, but I suppose I could understand that Ezra was merely trying to survive, too.

When my father wasn't home, I would occasionally bring up the beautiful sarongs he used to paint or the pencil drawings he would make of my mother and me. But even when my father wasn't in our presence, he wouldn't hear of it.

"Zoelle, please. I don't want to hear about that time ever again. Mother was too much of an influence on me, and I don't want anyone to know I ever engaged in such frivolity," he said with a razor-sharp tongue, his back stiff and his face cold and menacing.

I could tell it deeply saddened my mother to see Ezra turn into a miniature version of my father, but we both knew there was nothing we could do to prevent it from happening. It was as though my father had burrowed his hands inside my brother's skin and turned a light off.

But it wasn't only that Ezra's sweetness was gone. He also became a kind of mole for my father when he could no longer pursue the things that brought him the most pleasure; he started watching my every move in a way that felt invasive and stealthy. I no longer trusted he would keep any confidence. He had become a kind of home surveillance for the days my father was away. He was my father's eyes and ears, and although I didn't admit it, I experienced tremendous grief at how, seemingly overnight, my little Ezra was to never be seen again.

It had always been hard to sneak around with Hana—the town where we lived was small and filled with the expected gossip, and certainly any small town in Texas would not accept the love and intimacy Hana and I shared. Now that Ezra was my father's spy, it proved even more difficult. Because even without my father's invested interest in his half-Indonesian daughter, I knew what would happen if he ever discovered the depths of our relationship. It wasn't only because Hana was a girl. My father, even with an Indonesian spouse and child, would stop at nothing to keep us from engaging with anyone who shared our dark skin. That would have caused the most severe punishment. This was never spoken—it was obvious in the hateful language he spat out on the road or when discussing business.

One thing was clear: Ezra could never know about Hana. For both our sakes.

*

One day I woke up to a torrential rainstorm, and even though my mother hadn't risen yet, I knew she would be too struck with trepidation to drive us into town. My bag, which I'd thrown haphazardly on the ground the day before, opened slightly to reveal an old copy of *Lysistrata* Hana lent me a few days prior, suggesting it would help me in my research. I was in no rush to read it as I assumed, in my usual act of hubris, anything I hadn't found personally on my own could not offer me anything of substance, but I had accepted it from her so as not to hurt her feelings.

Still, I was bored waiting for the rain to dissipate, so I started to read it. I also wanted to be able to say something to Hana if she were to ask what I thought of her gift. To my surprise, reading this book reminded me of the study Hana had found that caused my first display of fitful rage, and what it would mean if, as a society, we became less dependent upon men for societal needs or even reproduction. Excited and unthinking, desperate to speak to anyone about my discovery, I ran to my mother after reading the book for a couple of hours. She was preparing a spicy Malay stew to feed us for lunch that day. I tried to explain to her my epiphany as she stirred the stew with a wooden spoon unthinkingly with one hand and held the book in the other as she read the synopsis that graced the back of the volume. She didn't even finish reading that much. She exclaimed nonchalantly without giving my thoughts much attention: "Aiyo, Zo. Why you read this silly book? No point, basically." She handed it back to me, her eyes barely looking up as she returned to the meal at hand.

Her reaction annoyed me. I was eager to find someone to talk out these exciting ideas with—and there was no way to call Hana without my mother or Ezra overhearing and asking questions. In a moment of vulnerability and intellectual fervor, I tried to reach out to Ezra.

"Ezzie, look!" I said, calling him by my old pet name for him without thinking. I could tell he wasn't amused, but nothing could have stopped me at that moment. "I prefer Ezra, please," he stated without looking up at me, and continued to read a book my father asked him to write a report on by the end of that weekend.

"Have you read this play? I wonder what it would be like not to depend on men the way we always have. What if, in the future, one could even have children without men entirely?" I blurted out, as though he was the old Ezra, the one I had spent all my childhood days with. It was a foolish mistake.

"Are you kidding? I often wonder who is filling your head with these ideas. Where you get these books from. Men will always matter. You'll see." With that, Ezra went back to his book without a second's glance back at me. I was incensed and devastated that there was no one with whom I could share my ideas when I was finally ready, that the two people I thought had been mine to cherish and love my whole life were slipping like sand through my fingers.

"What happened to you? You used to be my light. I don't know who—or what—you are now."

"Well, maybe it's time you stopped treating me like one of your childhood dolls," Ezra yawned, jotting down a note in his book. I stormed off and stewed in my room for days. No one noticed, or seemed to care. My mother left dinner trays for me outside my bedroom door. Eventually, loneliness and boredom got the best of me, and life proceeded as normal.

If my mother—or even Ezra—had offered a space for me to work out the ideas beginning to percolate in me after reading Aristophanes's satire, then perhaps she would have expressed a deeper concern that day in the kitchen, and we would not be here now, you and I, speaking of how my ideas ultimately led to my ruin. Instead, it only assured me that the people surrounding me were either not confident in my own abilities to surpass the innovations already performed by men or were disinterested in the kind of immersion in ideas I had already decided to devote my life to. There would no longer be anyone I could share these ideas with. It was around this time that, aside from Hana, I would develop an admittedly troubling habit of easily and promptly casting aside anyone I found no longer of use to me. My family and the small town in which we lived had exceeded their usefulness. It was time to move on.

But as I attempted to make my plans for the future, time went on, and my connection with Hana deepened over the succeeding months, even continuing back in the city during the school year. Hana and I had to rely on other forms of communication to share our ideas and curiosities (and at times, tender moments of desire for one another) surreptitiously. Although I greatly missed her during those periods, I must admit it was freeing to be able to focus more on my work without the constant distraction of Hana—of erotic needs, of making time. There was nothing keeping me from my higher purpose, from what I felt had been my destiny from birth.

Still, we continued to explore the ideas of other minds from afar, and began reading novels and critical texts that explored the dangerous power of men and other feminist ideals—we dug deep into Atwood and Butler, Wollstonecraft and Lorde, Rich and Carter. These writers imbued me with an ambition to reach for a pursuit deeper than that of a reader of giants and a potential future theorist in our little excitable pair. I wanted to penetrate the world and bestow on it something it had never been given before, just like so many men had done in decades past. It wasn't enough for me to write critically about gender and toxic masculinity or to ponder the future potential of science, like these women writers I admired and read voraciously and like Hana hoped to do after receiving her master's degree. Even though I did not have any great desire to carry a child or parent myself—my only model left me wondering if I could ever raise a child with love and acceptance—I was always contemplating how pairs like ours could reproduce without relying on a man (and being forced to accept all the conditions he would come with). What if I came up with a way to create an embryo and prove it could be carried to full term by a human without the need of men entirely? How unparalleled a voice I would embody next to all the men who could not discover anything even close to that kind of innovation!

Not long after this epiphany, my mother, Ezra, and I found ourselves on an unusual outing together. Uncharacteristically, my mother came into each of our rooms early in the morning and demanded we get dressed and meet her in the car. My father was in town for the weekend, and I suppose she was trying to get us out of the house before he woke. Shuffling our feet and rubbing our eyes, we managed to find our way to my father's car. I couldn't imagine what possible destination could be worth the backlash we would receive at home, having taken my father's precious mode of transportation. But since this was a side of my mother I hadn't seen before, I knew better than to question her.

We drove for two hours through West Texas. Each of us asked where we were headed, but my mother just snapped back, "You'll see. Quiet," and turned up the volume on her CD of various tracks of Indonesian monks chanting to the underscore of bells she often listened to when she wanted to relax. It promptly put us both to sleep.

I naturally woke up when the car came to a complete stop. She had taken us to Monahans Sandhills State Park, a public park covered in sand dunes I'd heard about for as long as we'd lived in West Texas, but I couldn't imagine either parent interested in visiting.

Standing next to the car, I stretched my legs and my back before taking in what stood before me. It was still early enough that the sun wasn't too harsh yet, and the predawn light allowed me to take in the stunning sight before me—sand as far as the eye could see. The wavy folds of sand in the enormous dunes looked like the ocean, and they brought me great comfort. My mother walked over to a nearby wooden bench, wearing a visor my grandmother had found at an Asian market in town, and began to read one of her beach reads. Ezra found himself a different bench, opening up his bag to return to our father's work that he had been asked to analyze by the next day. I rolled my eyes under my sunglasses.

I took off my sneakers and my socks, and I trudged through the sand. It felt good to work my legs after such a long drive, and I appreciated the ability to meditate on my own in such a tranquil environment. Because it was so early, the entire park was mostly deserted.

I walked up and down the massive sand dunes, but it was a struggle to walk against the wind, which whirred against my ears as I trudged along. I felt as though I were in a faraway land, something I read about in a storybook, perhaps *Arabian Nights*. At times my foot caught against some debris, and it was only then that I remembered that there had been a torrential rainstorm just a couple of days before, and I reasoned that the debris was left over from the violent weather patterns at a place so barren.

That's when I came upon this eerie sculpture in the sand. It was white, and at first, I mistook it for some kind of mollusk or maybe a fossil. But it seemed if it were a fossil, the park rangers would have confiscated it already and brought it to the authorities in charge of preservation. No, this had to be something else. It was the color of the sand, except maybe a shade darker, and it had uneven curves, like a strange kind of coral reef. But in the desert.

I was transfixed by it, and after I found the first of its kind, I spent the rest of the morning scouring the park for as many as I could find. My mother and Ezra were so used to my various investigations that they barely looked up from their reading to discover what I was digging for. They must have thought I was just a silly girl looking for clay at the bottom of a sandpit.

I threw the lot of them—maybe a good seven desert sculptures—into my backpack surreptitiously, hoping the park staff wouldn't see me and tell me to leave them in the sand. After we made the trek back home, I scurried off to my room while my mother and Ezra both tended to my father, giving him enough attention so he would spare them his outburst of anger. After a bit of research, I discovered the name for my new finding: *Fulgurite*, a glass tube that forms when lightning and sand meet. When lightning strikes sand, the bolt travels down through the sand until it depletes itself of its energy source. As a result, the sand melts into a glass tube along the path of the lightning. Because the sand dunes at the state park are so deep, the lightning strike can travel a few inches before exhausting itself of its energy. I'd never seen anything like it before, and I couldn't stop thinking about it. It was leading me to some sort of connection within my own work, and I was determined to figure out what that would be. It made me think more about the power of electricity to cut one body into two or to transform ether into a whole other shape that had never existed before.

It was from this witness I began to delve deeply into researchers who specialized in laser-assisted hatching and embryology. I gave up all my other pursuits, including the creative investigations I was exploring with Hana. I would not stop, I determined inwardly, until I could discover a way to create a life without the use of sperm. Perhaps there was a way, I questioned, that I could use a laser to sculpt an embryo out of material in ways we had never considered before.

When I look back, I can see it now—this young, excitable new mind desperately endeavoring to make a name for herself without thinking about the obstacles that prevented other minds from likewise discoveries. At times, Hana warned me not to get too ahead of myself, to think about some of the ethical concerns regarding the scientific direction I was headed, but she stopped when she realized all her efforts were in vain. Perhaps destiny would always dictate that this story would inevitably find me, as well as my destruction.

李

I ran away from home the summer before my seventeenth birthday. I was in love. Her name was Ko.

Ba was starting to catch on—at least, that's what I imagined was behind the interrogating looks he gave me over his glasses as he asked questions meant to have only one answer: *How's the school? You save money? When you get real job will you stop cutting the hairs?* I answered the questions as any dutiful child would—could it be a lie if you were merely doing whatever you could to survive?—but really, at the same time, I was doing what any teenager did—sneaking away to be with my first love.

Ko was mixed, like me. Her mother was Korean and her father was Colombian. Her complexion, tinged with brown and orange, reminded me of the mini terracotta soldier replicas Ba kept perfectly aligned on a bookshelf in the garage. But there was nothing uniform about Ko.

We met in a ceramics class at the queer arts center—a class I had asked the teacher to audit because I couldn't afford to pay for it out of pocket, offering in exchange to help sort the glazes and the clay, wipe down the benches where students made their works, wash out the kiln, scrub its wooden wheels. I arranged a meeting with the teacher a few days before the class started, sharing a portfolio with a few prints of film photographs of plaster sculptures I had made over the past couple of years. One in particular, a bust of Audre Lorde with her words etched into the bottom—*Your silence will not protect you.*—she was particularly taken with. A nonbinary Afro-Latinx femme, she briefly stopped to look up at me when she reached that image. It's my theory that print is the reason she agreed to the trade.

Even though the ceramics series was meant for artists of varying levels, the teacher had a considerable reputation in the community and attracted many advanced artists. That's why it didn't surprise me when Ko came in with her professional-grade denim apron complete with brown leather straps and tie in the back already well worn, covered in stains of various materials. There was something else about her, though, that gave me pause. Although I'd already come to terms with my queerness—I'd had a crush on my basketball coach who taught us PE in seventh grade, and I found myself more turned on by the heroines than the male leads when Ba would take me to the movies—I'd never really been taken with any girl in real life. Until Ko.

Sometimes you just know when you've met someone who knows something of your life. I could tell by looking at her that she was of mixed race, just like me, and I had a suspicion, by the way her eyes turned at the last minute in their corners or by the shape of her nose, that she might be part Asian, too. But, beyond those parallels, there was something about the way she worked that drew all of my attention to her—how she furrowed her brow as she smoothed the squat leg of her hand-formed elephant with a palette knife or pinched the trunk with her clipped fingernail to create folds in the skin. I recognized that extended attention towards taking material in your hands and mastering it into a new form, a new body. I knew what it was like to make of the body only what you wish and to throw out what didn't work for you, including the world that lived just at your periphery. Like Diane Arbus said, *What's left after what one isn't is taken away is what one is.*

As the series continued onward, images of Ko and her menageries of animal-human hybrids that had become the focus of her pursuit began to invade my dreams, both waking and nocturnal. I was content to let them stay that way, imagining I wouldn't pursue anything further with Ko, not even a friendship, because I was afraid of Ba's reaction when he found out. I knew he would never accept something so perverse in me. What point was there to get excited by the newness of possibility only to know it would never be mine? It was Ko that would awaken it in me on her own when I least expected it.

One day, midway through the class's duration, I was rinsing all the tools and organizing them to close the studio for the day. The teacher had entrusted me with the studio at this point, and so I often closed up on my own. I was so concentrated on my own duties I forgot Ko was still there, refining her project for the week, a dolphin torso with human legs and feet. As I began washing the last tool, I felt Ko next to me, her arm grazing my side as she washed that same knife I had seen her work with for weeks now. Caught off guard, I let out a little yelp and jumped backwards. Realizing she heard the sound I had made, I felt the heat rise to my face.

"Oh, sorry. I didn't mean to scare you. I just didn't want you to have to clean this one, too," she winked at me as she finished rinsing it off, giving the tool a confident shake or two to get the excess water out. I felt her arm linger next to my waist, just longer than a moment. The little black hairs on my arms stood straight up.

"No worries, you're good! I just didn't realize you were still there," I overcompensated, smiling back at her.

Her lips curved into a sly, knowing grin, oozing confidence. As I finished up the last of the dishes, and cleaned the floor, she sat on the edge of the counter, staring at me. I tried to hurry, just in case she happened to be waiting for me. I'd never asked out a girl before, so I wasn't quite sure how to proceed, but I also didn't want to miss my opportunity to spend time with Ko outside of class. Just the two of us. A dream I couldn't have imagined until then.

I never imagined she would make the first move.

"Hey, wanna grab a quick coffee around the street? I know a place that makes a killer black sesame latte." She smiled that sly grin again, holding the door open for me, tossing her thick mane of black hair to rest on her right shoulder. I melted inside.

That was the moment it all began—that summer turned my life into so many shades of color I never expected, nor had ever witnessed before.

Z

By the time I reached college age, I declared to my parents it was time for me to travel to the University of Oxford to attend a specialized program in reproductive science. Although I wasn't initially altogether certain either of my parents were convinced about the sustainability of embryology, they changed their tune when I showed them an informative pamphlet I received in the mail detailing the accelerated program at Oxford in which prospective students could receive both undergraduate and graduate degrees in reproductive science within the same amount of time it took a traditional student to receive their bachelor's in the United States. I was hesitant to travel so far away for my studies—I felt a certain degree of discomfort leaving my mother to my father's whims, even though I'd never been able to protect her from them, and Hana, who I couldn't imagine not having close to me for that long. But just before the date of my impending departure, it so happened that the universe would throw a wrench into my plans, the first great tragedy of my young life, a sign of the horrors to come.

But even before that, one of my worst fears would come true my last summer at the country house.

As I grew into my nonbinary identity, it became increasingly difficult to carry the articles of clothing from these two lives back and forth in my backpack (I would have preferred a brown leather satchel, but alas, that was too masculine to get away with around my father and Ezra) without drawing too much attention to myself. Early in our time together, Hana and I found this glorious deep emerald trunk we buried in the ground in this abandoned yard near our secret hiding place. It was the perfect makeshift locker for the clothing I would wear on my dates with Hana, and a convenient place to keep the clothes I would wear back to the house so that my family wouldn't be the wiser.

As time went on, I would find all kinds of clothing items to help me understand the ways in which I wanted to dress—contemporary vests and waistcoats I wore over colorful button-down shirts, silk scarves I tied around my neck like my father's neckties, button suspender pants with leather suspenders to match, even fedoras and baseball caps that made me look like a boy when seeing my trousers and short fade from behind. I would often be called sir as someone passed me on the sidewalk or alerted me I'd dropped something on the ground. For those few moments before the person saw me on the other side and saw my feminine face, it would make my heart flutter to have the calalai in me recognized.

I had a ritual that was comforting but also thrilling: I

would sneak over to the abandoned grounds and gather my outfit for the afternoon, sometimes changing what was already waiting for me if I felt Hana had seen it too many times in a row. For just a few hours, I would toss aside my form-fitting tank tops and snug denim, my jade earrings and silk headbands. I would change behind a copse of trees. Sometimes Hana and I left little gifts for each other in the trunk before meeting—I would leave her gold bangles and books I knew she would love, and she would leave me seersucker bowties and notebooks with leather flap-tie closures to organize all of my ideas.

But, as always happens with secrets, the longer you get away with them, the harder they are to keep safe.

As the weeks passed, I grew increasingly confident that Hana and I were safe in our little bubble in the town square, so safe it felt we were invisible to all except each other. It felt as though the universe had shielded us from the forces set to keep us apart, including my brother who was once so dear to me but who had become just another version of my father, except even worse somehow because I had once allowed myself to be vulnerable to him.

It was foolish, but of course, it is human nature that once the threat does not imminently appear, you believe you've gotten away with it.

I had stopped looking over my shoulder every few seconds to see if Ezra or my father was behind me. Besides, by then Ezra was often in town with my father, desperate to please him and learn the family business to take it over someday. I had stopped checking to see if any of my father's business associates or Hana's mother were nearby as we kissed in secret but out in the open in our hiding place behind the trees.

Then one day, I knelt next to the ground I had touched so many times before. The ground was soft, as though it had already been cut open by some other tool, some other visitor. I stroked the ground next to our burial place with my hand. Its softness was not comforting to me. I tried to shake it off, telling myself I was having one of those moments you have when you randomly become hyperaware of the world around you. Perhaps Hana had dug up the trunk shortly before our meeting to leave me one of her customary gifts. Besides, who else could possibly know our secret place in the dirt?

I took the small trowel out of my backpack as always, and dug until I unearthed the trunk. My hands were shaking so violently I struggled to open the latch. Hana and I had never thought to buy a lock for it because there was never any need to. I almost couldn't believe what I found when I lifted the trunk out of its hole in the ground and opened it.

The trunk was empty.

My heart began to clang in my chest like faulty machinery.

All that remained was just one folded piece of paper with my name written on the top. As I lifted it uneasily to a reading distance, I immediately recognized the penmanship. Ezra, that wonderful darling boy with the golden ringlets, my cherished treasure. Until Pa stole him away with his cruelty.

The note only had one line inside: *See you at home, Ez.* I instantly burst into tears, thinking of how informal he attempted to make his assault on my life and the intimacies that mattered so much to me. I didn't have time to place the trunk back into the dark earth. I anxiously shoved the note into my jeans pocket and ran to find Hana.

I had arrived a bit earlier than our meeting time because I always liked to have extra time to don my true gentlemanly skin for her. As anxiety shot in waves down the course of my body, my breath spurted out in rapid puffs from my lungs. The very reason I needed my legs to work in hyperdrive was why they were determined not to; the anxiety turned my legs into gelatinous mush attached to my waist. It became hard to run at the pace I needed to so that I could get to Hana and she could tell me what to do or at least calm me down. If I could make it to her, I thought to myself, I would be all right.

Hana saw me through the glass wall attached to the door of the independent bookstore, where I always found her. I could tell she knew something was wrong by the way she dropped the books she was holding in her hands and ran out of the bookstore to meet me.

"Z?" she started, a look of concern falling across her face, her brows bending to meet one another.

"I . . . the trunk . . . empty . . . Ezra," I managed to get out between accelerated breaths. She responded with a look of confusion. Since I still couldn't speak, I tore into my pocket and threw the note at her chest, more aggressively than I intended from fear and urgency.

The seconds it took for her to read the note felt achingly slow and long, as though the entire scene unfolding was submerged underwater. Then I saw her face slowly put the pieces together and match mine in anxiety and fear, which offered some strange sense of validation, a feeling I was no longer alone in it, even though I knew it was I who would pay the consequences.

"Oh, Z—" she cried out, and pressed me against her chest. I tried to fight against her aims to soothe me.

"How can you possibly understand what this is like? Your parents—" I snapped back at her, resentful at how alone I felt, but Hana pressed her mouth against my ear and instructed me to inhale and exhale, her sweet breath calming me down whether I wanted to or not. I gradually felt my heart recede in my chest and my pulse quiet in my wrist. As the adrenaline coursing through my veins became softer and softer, I held onto her harder and harder, knowing it could very well be the last time I would see her.

I was afraid to return home. But I knew I would have to face what stood on the other side of my front door sooner or later. I just didn't know if the monster behind the door was my father, as it had always been, or Ezra, my love, my brethren, my friend. Of course, he had been taken from me already. But I had still not wanted to fully admit it to myself. This was certainly the last way I wanted to be reminded of that fact.

This time when I took my leave of Hana, I held her for so long, so much longer than I ever had before, because we both knew we might never see each other again. I touched her cheek just as she reached for my same cheek, and we stood like that for the longest, staring lovingly into one another's eyes.

The world is full of uncertainty, but it is not quite the same as when one knows the uncertainty that lies within their grasp.

What I hoped for when I reached our summer home: An empty driveway and street in front of the house. A house empty of my father. An Ezra who would pretend the incident with the trunk never happened, that my clothes were stored somewhere safe by the boy I used to love so tenderly—under my bed perhaps, or deep in my closet. I conjured these visions in my mind so forcefully it made my head hurt, and I feared I would wrinkle my brow permanently. Of course, I knew they would never come true. These types of dreams or close calls never happened for girl-boys like me. Not with white fathers like mine.

My father's car was parked in the driveway, as though it had always been there. For but a moment, I stared at the house—its palatial white columns, its soft red brick, its long, brick walkway, the massive trees planted on the grass grown on both sides. It was dusk, and the light was orange in the sky, matching the warm lamps lit inside the house. How quaint the image appeared. How dishonest the architecture, the sweetness of the interior light seemed, knowing what was awaiting me. I walked slow and steady down the walkway, or at least tried to, as though I were walking towards my doom. In a way, I was.

My mother and grandmother were not in the living room with Ezra and my father when I shut the front door behind me.

My father sat in his usual place, at his large beige armchair where he watched television on the rare nights he would stop working. Ezra sat on the couch next to him, his upper torso leaning towards my father, while my father leaned backwards in the chair. Ezra looked up when he saw me. My father's chair was facing away from me, so he didn't see me enter. But he undoubtedly was waiting for me and must have seen Ezra's eyes notice me.

"Zoelle, is that you?" he offered, as though he were not the father that he was.

"Yes, it's me," I said as casually as I could. I didn't want to make a false assumption. Maybe Ezra would just use the trunk and its contents as a threat to hold over my head forever. Wishful thinking was the only thing keeping me intact.

"Come, sit down," he wheeled his chair around so he could see me, and then pointed towards the sofa, next to Ezra.

When I came around the side of my father and approached the sofa, I saw it. A small plastic crate filled with the contents from the trunk, taunting me from the glass coffee table on which the crate rested. A note from Hana, the envelope's seal broken. My favorite velvet vest, my patterned suspenders, my wool trousers. I tried not to let any expression show on my face. My father appeared strangely calm, perhaps because he didn't actually care.

"I am glad to see you, Zoelle. I take it these things are yours?" He peered at my face.

"Y-yes, sir," I deferred, taking my seat as far away from Ezra as I could, too enraged by his betrayal to even look him in the eye, even though he tried to make eye contact with me.

"What is the meaning of this?" My father placed his hands delicately in his lap, but I knew better. I knew what my father was. He hadn't convinced me of his mercy, not even in the slightest. It was actually more unsettling that my father wasn't flying off the handle like he usually did with my mother, and I recalled how he had been with Ezra just a year before. I knew that each action was a move forward in the game of strategy we now played with one another, and I had best pick my move carefully.

"I just enjoy wearing them. I keep them in the place Ezra found them because I only wear them when I am in town," I said calmly, measured. Maybe all that mattered was my calalai, not Hana. One could dream.

"I see. And who do you wear them for?"

"Myself, mainly." I hadn't lied, yet. I wouldn't offer anything not directly asked of me about Hana.

"Hm," he said, standing up and walking over to the crate. He rifled through the various items until he got to the note from Hana. Opening the envelope, he pulled the note out with his long, thin fingers, and read through it. It made me sick to think that my father would ever hold anything so intimate between us in his hands, reading words meant only for me. I did my best to hide my innermost feelings.

"Then who is this Hana?" he asked, pronouncing her name incorrectly. Perhaps intentionally.

"Her name is Hana," I said, correcting him. At that, he threw the note down with the envelope, his eyes red and menacing. Before I knew it, he was staring at me just inches away from where I sat. I looked up at his blue eyes, sharp like piercing metal.

"Stand up!" he spat into my face. I stood up quickly, quietly.

"You dare to correct me? When you have been lying and behaving like this all this time? What is it with the two of you? What did I do to deserve such perverse spawn?" He looked briefly at Ezra, who held his head down in shame. "You," he said, his attention and focus back on me, "are my own flesh and blood. And you still are so shameful. You disgust me." He leaned forward, and smacked me in the face. The strike of his hand against the silence inside the house rang like two pieces of wood slapping against one another in one clean sound. My hand instinctively met my cheek, stinging and pulsating in pain, as I cried out once, and then held the pain against my tongue, remaining silent. He looked curiously at me.

"Well, I will just do what I did with the evidence of Ezra's monstrosity. I will burn it in the backyard. But I want you to watch me do this, so you will know never to do this again," my father said, the heat retreating in his voice. "Ezra, thank you for your service. Your job is done here. Please go to your room and prepare for our meeting tomorrow." Ezra nodded deferentially and left the room.

My father and I walked outside together. As ordered, I carried the crate out to the backyard. The tin pail had been returned to where it usually sat on the deck, and I watched as those precious keepsakes that felt most true of my heart were burned against the blackness of the dark night.

I never forgave my mother for her silence, or her inaction. We never spoke of it.

*

Shortly after the incident with the trunk, Ezra, who was now reaching his midteens, mysteriously caught measles. It was only when my mother pressed my father about how Ezra could have possibly caught such a serious illness at such a late and unexpected age that my father admitted neither he nor Ezra had been vaccinated. I had been vaccinated as a small child, several years before my father brought Ezra into our lives. Only with Ezra's contraction of the illness did I learn that my mother's choice to vaccinate me was a source of contention between my parents—my father's parents had also chosen not to vaccinate my father. They believed not only that it was unimaginable that their child could become contaminated with such communicable diseases, but that the vaccine itself was a poison no longer necessary as these diseases, *barbarian*, as my father's parents called them, had already fallen away with the modern trends of sanitation and hygiene. My father was convinced modern vaccinations were just another way for doctors to take his money.

Despite how abusive and unkind our father had been over the years, he and Ezra had become quite close since the fire incident. When he heard that Ezra had taken ill that summer, my father took several weeks off of work and moved back into the summer house with us full time while Ezra was in recovery. Seeing Ezra in such a tormented state sent my father into a severely distraught condition. But I knew it wasn't only because of Ezra's well-being he was suddenly so concerned, but also because Ezra was the child he had invested so much time and effort into teaching the family business to so he could take it over one day. As the illness began to take its course, and Ezra's body became polka-dotted with small, red spots across his neck, arms, legs, and feet, it became impossible to keep my father away from him. At first, my father submitted to our warnings that Ezra needed to stay strictly quarantined inside of his room with no visitors and only receive soups, water, and medicines outside his door. But given that my father had always seen Ezra as a reflection of his own image and that he still believed he was immune to such infectious diseases, he could not sustain his distance. While my mother and I were at the market gathering more ingredients for Ezra's daily soup and my grandmother was taking a nap, my father stole into Ezra's room with a cool washcloth and a glass of water. Ezra coughed on my father's hand when he placed the cloth on his forehead. Within a matter of days, my father became very ill.

Although Ezra was young enough to ultimately heal from the virus, my father was not so lucky. On his deathbed, my father joined Ezra's hands together with mine and declared a destiny that would intertwine our lives forever. I imagine he saw the vow he asked from us as a blessing; I would soon realize it was a curse, the very curse of my fateful future. I would realize it was not only our future happiness he demanded, but that he wanted his thriving business to never leave the hands of our family through the possible manipulations of another spouse. "Ezra and Zoelle," he began in a low, raspy voice through dry coughs, "I know I have not been the perfect father, but even still, I hate to leave you while your lives are just beginning. There is only one thing I ask. Please marry once you become of marrying age. This is the only way I can be assured the business will stay within our family. Zo, you certainly cannot marry that dreadful woman from town. The world will never approve. Know that my eternal peace rests on your union. Please do not deny me this request. I beg you. Zoelle, as the daughter, you must help your mother now. Ezra, you must take my place as the man of the house and provide for your cousin, your friend, your bride. I hope to see you in the afterlife, joined together as I join you now. Do not forsake me after all I've done for you." With that, my father fell into a deep slumber from which he did not wake.

I did not feel much grief seeing my father die, as he had only been a tyrant to me, had transformed my brother from who he was meant to be, and had waged terror daily on my mother. I was more concerned with how Ezra would respond to this ridiculous demand. I tried to measure Ezra's reaction to this deathbed plea, but when I looked over at Ezra, his eyes were clouded with tears. He didn't make any move to speak to me or even glance my way. He held my father's hand so tight I thought he might never let go.

For several days my mother stayed in her room, and the entire house carried her as she wept. I imagine at times she wept out of grief for a man who gave her this life of comfort and privilege, but I wonder if she also wept out of relief he could no longer turn her into an object on which to project the complexity of his rage and ego. Due to our father's recent and heightened adoration of Ezra, exacerbated by the guilt he felt over having inadvertently caused our father to become ill, Ezra fell into a deep state of despair. By the time my father died, I had come to terms with what my father had been (as well as what he could never become) although I could acknowledge, at the very least, how unfortunate it was that my father had died before living a full life. But I was much more concerned with what would come of this promise he had determined Ezra and I fulfill. Soon I would depart for England, and given how deeply Ezra felt our father's loss, I grew worried this vow would become an obstacle preventing me from achieving my ambitions. I couldn't help but think about Hana and what was possible in our future. Of what would be foretold by my father's wishes. Would he control my life even from the grave?

Before I left for England, I knelt on the floor next to my mother's bedside, anxious about my father's words: It was now my obligation to support my mother in the chores he always saw as strictly women's work, such as cleaning, cooking, and managing the house.

"Ma?" I gently touched her shoulder, afraid to wake her, even though she was constantly in bed at that time, processing her grief.

"Yes, Zoelle, what is it?" she mumbled, her eyes closed as she lay on her back without moving or making any effort to rise to a seated position.

"Pa told me I needed to stay home and help—" I started, but she interrupted me before I could finish, sitting up quickly.

"Zoelle, come into bed with me." She patted the space next to her. I crawled in, an unusual moment of closeness between us.

"No. I do not need help. Zoelle, you are the one to prove to me why I married your father and came all this way to this new life and sacrificed so much happiness. Please, I beg you, go England, do wonders with that smart brain," she said, tapping her finger lovingly on my forehead.

"Do something with what your father gave us working so hard, learn great things, do great things. Okay? Ezra will chase your father dreams forever. I can't stop him. Please, stay few more days, then go Oxford to big college, okay?" I held her, a rare moment of affection between us. It was more than she had ever spoken to me. I imagined it was a lot for her. I didn't take it lightly.

I delayed my trip for several days out of concern for Ezra, even though he never spoke to me, waiting to make sure he had moved through enough of his grief to withstand my departure. Even after everything, it was still hard to leave him in this much pain. I spent most of my remaining days in Texas with Hana, now that I no longer had to look over my shoulder. Ezra looked at me coldly when he would see me leave the house, but I didn't care. We both knew there was nothing he could do to me. I tried to convince Hana to come with me to Oxford to study literature while I pursued biomedical sciences, but she couldn't bear to leave her parents behind for that long. I didn't have the heart or energy to even argue that her parents always managed to come first.

We met late the night before my departure when Ezra, my mother, and grandmother were in the depths of their slumber. I had received a large inheritance from my father's death, and I spent a tiny portion of that money renting a room for us at a local inn not far from the center of town. It was on this night we finally consummated our great respect and love for one another. We spent all night together. The next morning, even as the sun rose in the sky, it was impossible to tear myself away from her.

I had already confided in Hana about my father's deathbed promise; but we were young and full of idealism and imagined a world in which this promise would not have to be kept, that defying the promise would not come with any serious consequences. How foolish we were! The only promise I cared about was the one I made to Hana, that we would write to one another about our discoveries and inquiries. Hana vowed to come up with a way to visit me before the end of my first quarter. That night as we cuddled under blankets and talked with one another like girls and newly beloveds, we fantasized about what time together away from our families and anything we found familiar could be like. The next morning, I promised myself I would write to Ezra, even though he was no longer the sweet and delicate tender heart I had remembered for so long. I wondered, since my father's influence over Ezra was fairly new, if I could bring back the old Ezra with my missives and memories of the sweet boy from before. However, the grief had already turned his demeanor and disposition even colder, and he was more removed than he already had been. I hoped it was not too late. Of course, I secretly wished that if I could get through to him, maybe I could convince him to forget about fulfilling my father's promise. As I gave my farewells, he offered me a melancholy and formal goodbye kiss on each cheek in silence, his eyes two gray portals that I feared led only to a blankness or an obsession to fulfill his father's demand to somehow make the pain of his loss less starkly felt. But, I didn't give that fear too much mind. Although I was deeply sad to leave Hana, I was much too excited about the journey awaiting me at the other end of that long flight and all the greatness that I expected lay just within reach.

I had a need to feel I was somewhat sturdy in nature and disposition. In our family structure, when we were younger, it was little Ezra who was prone to fits of vulnerability and tenderness, whereas I always held my heart rather tight to my sleeve. However, on the seemingly endless flight to England, I allowed myself to indulge in the abject despondency I felt in being so alone and isolated from everyone and everything I knew. Not only would I make my way through the world on my own for the first time, but I would no longer have Hana to accompany me on my intellectual quests. Even though I was too proud to admit that there was anything she could show me I didn't already know, I had become attached to our way of sharing ideas and writers and having someone I could share my latest inquiries with. I was also worried I would find myself surrounded in a sea of white, unfamiliar classmates with whom I would share no commonalities or interests. Over the past few years, I had grown very dependent on Hana and couldn't imagine any stranger supporting me as she had. Plus, I reflected to myself as the passengers to the left and right of me slumbered through the journey over land and ocean, I couldn't imagine a scenario in which anyone's mind would match my own.

Thoughts like these eventually prompted me to nod off for the last few hours of the flight, until at last, I woke to a view through the plane's small window: The steeples I remembered from the images I found of Oxford during my research. My roommate met me at the airport. His name was Henry, and he had a dark head of black hair and a distinctly Chinese face. Although I imagined he came directly from the mainland and thus would be more conservative in his approach to research and cohabitation than I would prefer, his face immediately put me at ease. We took a car to our dormitories, where I threw my baggage at the foot of my small bare mattress and fell into an immediate and deep slumber.

李

Ko smelled of lavender and Tide. Sometimes, when I kissed her at night, I could still taste a faint mixture of sauces on her tongue that I imagined garnished her dinner just hours before—hoisin, soy, sesame, fish, hot mustard. And always that added touch of kimchi, her favorite snack for any time of day. We shared boba and Korean barbecue together and stories of the annoying white liberals in Vermont. When we first met, I learned that one of my favorite pastimes—count the POCs—was a game she played, too. We compared how many plastic bags our parents kept under the sink, plastic containers above the stove that once held takeout pho from the one Vietnamese restaurant in town. What a gift it was to share time with someone who knew something of what my life was like. Before Ko, I'd never been kissed by anyone before. Boys stayed away from me, which I was grateful for; besides, I was lucky enough to have a boy's shape (boxy waist, flat chest, broad torso) so as not to attract them anyway.

By the time I learned enough about myself to know it was the shape, scent, and feel most often ascribed to girls that made my skin itchy with want and curiosity, I was old enough to realize if I approached the wrong one, things could get scary. I asked out a girl once at a café, where I had been sketching for hours. She was a barista and had silky black hair that fell halfway down her back, eyes shaded turquoise with dramatic eyeliner, and an understated but stylish look. The way her bottom hugged the back seat of her jeans excited me. I wanted to finger her curves. I stayed until closing hours, and when I walked out of the café to my car, I saw the barista standing next to the dumpster, emptying the trash. It was late. The sky was black, lit minimally with just a few streetlights sporadically placed by the sidewalks. When I walked up to see if she wanted someone to walk her to her car, she smiled at me. Initially, I thought the smile was for me, but I realized only too late it was for her boyfriend who came up to me from behind and threw me in a chokehold, shouting slurs and threats. That was the last time I ever approached a girl.

Even though Ba cropped my hair short, a style identical to his own, and made me wear his hand-me-down jeans he kept from his boyhood days, I was smart enough to know that didn't mean he'd accept *this.* I knew he didn't care whose body I lay with in the sweaty dark night, not really. What mattered more was what the 阿姨[22] and the 叔叔[23] and the future employers saw when they looked at me. That I represented him. What

---

22 āyí—aunt
23 shúshu—uncle

they saw must be like everyone else. He didn't leave everything he knew behind to come to America only for me to be so ungrateful as to want what was against nature and the world. I knew what he would say. *Life not fair. Just the way it is. We can't always have what we want.* He never said this to me directly. He didn't have to.

By the time the ceramics class ended, Ko and I were as entwined as a strand of DNA—a coil of endless togetherness. Somehow, no matter how much time we spent together, hiding out in libraries or cuddling on a blanket in all the city parks we'd convinced ourselves were safe, it was never enough for either of us. We could both feel the pressure build as we tried to make the impossible happen. The more we clutched to each other for survival, away from Ba and Ko's parents, the closer the threat of discovery came.

Ba ultimately made our decision for us. Even if he didn't realize it.

One day, I was out with Ko and lost track of time. I came home fifteen minutes late for dinner. My lies didn't measure up, but hard as he tried to squeeze the deeper truth out of me, I wouldn't reveal what he would see as a sick, twisted black mark. I just couldn't. I can still feel the pieces of plaster that splintered my back as Ba slammed me against the dining room wall, our stir-fry and 牛尾湯[24] going cold.

"Tell me now. Where were you? Who you with? Some

---

24 niúwěi tāng—oxtail soup

boy? Who?" With each word, another slam, another reinforcement I would never be able to tell him it was Ko who confettied the world with peonies, their pinks tickling my skin. If he was like this about a boy, I couldn't imagine what he would be like if he learned I'd snuck off with a girl. I shuddered to even think of it.

Before long, he exhausted himself and went to bed, shouting 討厭[25] to no one in particular, although I knew it was a curse meant only for me. I wouldn't discover what it actually meant until much later. I always assumed it meant some version of *bad girl* or *disobedient*, or some other term for a misbehaving child. Later, I asked a fluent Chinese American I knew if she was familiar with the expression. She told me there wasn't an exact English equivalent. But I saw the *O* of shock her mouth formed that she tried to quickly disguise when I revealed it was my ba who called me that every time he scolded me, often with no words to accompany it, just the heat of rage-tinged touch. That face alone motivated me to look it up in the English-Mandarin dictionary at the library sitting next to Ko one afternoon. It had never occurred to me to do so before. Perhaps I was too afraid to know the barbs he was willing to prick me with. Even if he didn't know that the secret I held was carved with the body of a girl, that moment alone convinced me he would always see this egg I tried to hold so carefully against my chest (so as not to ruin it) as foul, monstrous.

---

25 tǎo yàn—to loathe with disgust

Ko read over my shoulder, and after we both read the same words, that it meant to *loathe someone* or *look at a person with disgust*, she held my hand underneath the table, resting her head against my shoulder.

"Oh, Plum," she whispered in my ear. "I'm so sorry." She understood.

I knew then what I had to do.

Z

From the first moment of the first day of coursework through to the end of my accelerated master's degree in reproductive science, I was singularly focused, to the point of obsession, in learning as much as I could about the past and present technological advances of creating life. Although I dutifully attended my classes and met with my (all white male) professors as required, I found their teachings most rudimentary. Most of the knowledge I acquired during that time that truly mattered to me was self-taught, and it was this acquisition in which I became most invested. My roommate, Henry, tried to invite me to study sessions with the other students or to share pints of beer with him and his girlfriend, but he quickly learned I had no interest in any kind of social discourse or friendship; simply put, I had no time for such trivialities. The rest of the students in my cohort learned this about me within a matter of a few weeks. Since most of them were from somewhere in the United Kingdom, I assume they misread my peculiar behavior as being particularly American and didn't take it personally. If anything, this misperception only made it easier for me to pursue my own intellectual curiosities and suffer fewer distractions.

It was the professors themselves that were the least prepared to deal with me. I surpassed all academic expectations, which, unsurprisingly, impressed the faculty in the department, especially when I transitioned into my graduate work after receiving a Bachelor's of Science in their accelerated track; however, it quickly became clear to most of the faculty I had no interest in anything they could offer me. I found them, for the most part, conservative and slow in their willingness to experiment with the latest reproductive technologies. I, on the other hand, was so impassioned by my ambitions that I didn't see the dangers of my own impatience and haste for laboratory technology to catch up with my idealistic spirit.

I remember a particular exchange with Dr. Sullivan, my professor in IVF topics, during an open seminar on the latest innovations regarding in vitro fertilization technologies and ethical dilemmas. I had spent most of the course arguing with him, insisting that my perspective on the future of reproductive technology was the only way to see it and that progress always mattered more than ethical concerns. Many class sessions would devolve into heated debates between the two of us to the extent that even the other students halted any interjections they might have thought of offering to the conversation.

Then, just before finals, at the end of one particular class session, Dr. Sullivan asked in a forced nonchalance to see me after class. The students looked over at me with intrigue and worry in their eyes; but, as I had not formed intimate attachments with any of them, I found their concerns rather invasive. After a few minutes, just Dr. Sullivan and I remained in the small classroom. I walked to the front of the room, where he sat at a desk just in front of the blackboard still marked with his notes for that day's session.

"You wanted to see me?" I said without much thought. I believed he had nothing especially insightful to offer and having to stay after was merely a waste of my time. Dr. Sullivan stood up from his desk and pushed his chair back so that he could walk over to where I stood. He had a full head of salt-and-pepper hair, thick spectacles, and he wore a worn black suit with a dusty layer of chalk coating his lapels. Dr. Sullivan placed his spectacles in the pocket of his blazer, and rubbed his temples with his fingers, a move I had seen him perform many times when the two of us became embroiled in a heated debate.

"Zoelle," he said, looking me over in my suspenders and trousers, my thin patterned tie and crisp white Oxford shirt (now that I was so far from home and my father was long gone, I found no reason to hide my true nature). Being called Zoelle had always made me cringe, and so, as I had done many times before, I corrected him.

"Z. If you would, Professor Sullivan," I interrupted as he leaned his bottom against the edge of his desk. The disruption caught him off guard.

"Oh yes, I apologize. Z," he corrected, running a hand

through his hair.

"Is something the matter with my academic performance? What's the issue? I'd love to get back to my room and work on my own res—" I began, but Dr. Sullivan interrupted me.

"Yes, Z. This is exactly why I want to speak to you." He motioned for me to sit in one of the desks closest to his own. I sat down at the very edge of the seat, my legs thrust in front of me, taking a quick look at my watch, a gesture meant to indicate I didn't intend to waste much time speaking to a professor who I had already surpassed in wisdom and insight.

"Look. I know exactly where you are. I was there once, too." He smiled, looking into the distance past me. "But what we try to offer here is a space for you to explore these exciting ideas and ambitions while also warning you of what lies just ahead. These dilemmas we face in this course should not be taken lightly. I hope you can appreciate that and spend some time considering that perhaps your faculty know the risks that come with reproductive science. Be wary of believing you can outwit Nature," he said with a wink, fixing a steadfast gaze on me in hopes it would penetrate.

"I appreciate your feedback and concern," I said curtly, offended that anyone believed they could teach me anything about a field I had conquered as a young child.

"Please think about what I've said. IVF and stem cell research come with many ethical issues. It is simply not possible for a burgeoning student to have a thorough understanding of their hazardous potential. Believe me. You'll see. I just hope you learn this before it's too late," Dr. Sullivan tried one last time, and then sighed as I nodded silently and excused myself from the classroom.

I wish I could say I took what Dr. Sullivan and my other graduate faculty said to heart, that I questioned my own ego and belief in my intellectual prowess. I see now that my professors were trying to warn me, in a similar manner I now hope to urge you to take caution. So much of ethical restraint lies far beyond the technological possibility of science. In other words, just because science enables us to perform a particular advancement in the development of new life doesn't mean we should. I hope, for your sake, you don't learn the hard way, like I did.

At some point during this very exciting period of intensive focus and inquiry, Hana wrote to me incredibly pleased that she had discerned a way to visit me at Oxford with her parents' blessing. I was delighted to receive her letter, as I was eager to share with her all I had uncovered in the years since our last reunion. But then something happened that caused me to refrain from replying to her missive and request at the last minute.

By complete happenstance, I came upon an article that reported a pioneering experiment in which the scientist used the stem cells from the skin of mice in order to create an embryo without using either egg or sperm. To the scientist's complete astonishment, the embryo did, indeed, implant in the womb of the mouse, and the mouse gave birth to a healthy mouse pup. In order to do this, they basically injected the embryo with genetic material in order to confuse the body into believing it was an embryo that consisted of both female and male chromosomal material.

Unsurprisingly, the scientist cautioned against being too excited about what this experiment could mean for the future of creating human life for queer couples, those who desired to have children without a partner, or people with vaginas interested in having children past child-bearing age who were considered too old for fertility treatment. What this technology could lead to, the scientist warned, was what he called *designer fertility*, in which a person could find stealthy ways to come into the possession of the stem cells of a candidate they found a desirable genetic parent without consent. As you might predict, I did not heed the article's warning. Instead, I felt as though a ray of light had permeated the darkness of my isolation. You also must understand that, at that point in my life, I had found men only provided my life with a sense of powerlessness. So, even thinking back on it now, I can see I felt a kind of urgency to find a way that a person with a vagina could further their own genetic line without needing to rely on cis men whatsoever.

Please remember that I am not recounting the delusions of an unwell person. It is true we do indeed have the technology to need neither egg nor sperm to create life. After many excruciatingly exhausting hours of study and experiments, I finally discovered I was able to create a child using any kind of genetic material I could find. Further, I learned I could inject the material to physically imprint whatever details I desired in this child—height, weight, muscle mass, eye color, hair color, skin complexion, etc. The entire future of human perfection lay, quite literally, at my fingertips.

I can say that perhaps there was something of my own father in my itchy push towards this discovery. From my vantage point, my entire existence was owed to a man but also burdened by his sense of what he was owed on his very deathbed. He aimed to do to me what he had done to my mother, to force me into a life with someone I did not love. My mother had merely left one servitude for another, and what made matters worse was the knowledge that she did this for me, to provide a life for her children she could never have as a poor, working child of a single mother. Perhaps I wanted to prove to myself that I didn't need a man to do anything, not even to create human life. I urgently hoped Hana and I would be able to create a life together, somewhere, somehow, especially now that my father was gone. We wouldn't even need to count on a man to donate his sperm to us. We wouldn't have to wonder if, at any moment, he would return, as men often do, to take back what they felt was theirs to possess. As I became so singularly focused on how I could change the course of reproductive science forever, as well as chart my own legacy, it completely slipped my mind that Ezra might still be giving this deathbed request any heed whatsoever.

To say I delighted in the power of my discovery is an understatement. I foresaw no obstacle to my goal, and in fact, the visions that occupied my thoughts and dreams constellated mostly on the future progeny of my design. I saw myself as a benevolent God who could create complex, flawless, mixed race, nonbinary creatures. They would be the ideal combination of all the best parts of human life and embodiment. Like Frederick Douglass predicted in *The Future of the Colored Race* in 1886, *Races and varieties of the human family appear and disappear, but humanity remains and will remain forever.*

I can see by the way you lean forward and the sparkle in your eyes that you're hoping I'll tell you the secret behind the technology I discovered and through which I made a name for myself. You're trying to be coy, but I've been at this a while. I can see it in the quick flutter of your eyes, the rapid breath you think I can't hear. Certainly, I, above all others, can empathize with the power of another's ambition on which you hope to model your own future progress and success. But I would be hard-pressed to find a single listener of this story who would feel the same eagerness upon hearing the end of my tale. I cannot, in good faith, lead you to a path of destruction, as has happened to me. Please, I beg you, as I recount to you what led to my tragedy, learn from my example how dangerous knowledge that goes unquestioned is and how much more fulfilled and content the person who creates within the world, and not beyond it and Nature, is.

I did experience a few days here and there in which I engaged in late-night episodes of extreme self-doubt, uncertain as to whether I should pursue this technology of creating what I conceived of as the perfect human life. Although I had acquired the knowledge and skills to achieve what I was after, it was still an incredibly new and as yet unverifiable technology for humans. Because I knew that colleagues in the field, fellow classmates, or even faculty members, would only seek to prevent me from this work, there was not a single soul I could speak to about this venture, which at times, left me in a state of anxiety. At first I wondered if I should only experiment with getting rid of sperm specifically but stick to fertilizing an embryo with a woman's egg, but as you can imagine, I was too enthralled with the possibilities of my vision and discovery to stop short. Besides, I rationalized, if I drew back from my initial idea, wouldn't I just be like all those others I had judged previously for not pursuing science to the farthest ambition? I was completely convinced that nothing could stand in my way, that I had absolute control and oversight over this project at hand. I did not consider for a second all of the possible obstacles that could have kept me from achieving my perfect being.

What I did know was that I could not use someone else's laboratory or provisions in order to make this being. I had to be in absolute control and hold sovereignty over every aspect of the experiment. I also did not want there to be any opportunity for another scientist to steal my ideas and take credit for the many years of work that had come to fruition in this new venture. I still had a small set of funds left over from the inheritance I acquired when my father passed. I used the inheritance to purchase land and develop the laboratory you know well, which provided the site of your position and the occasion for us to meet. As I began to hire technicians, interns, and supervisors to manage the lab—and to hopefully bring in funding that could support future endeavors—I developed a restricted wing that would be off-limits to every single person but me. It was heavily secured with a key card and a code that only I have access to. *Life and death appeared to me ideal bounds that I should first break through and then pour a torrent of light into our dark world. A new species would bless me as its creator and source; many happy and excellent natures would owe their being to me.*[26] I could already imagine all the queer and non-normative parents who would feel endless gratitude for what I had been able to give them. It is from this hopeful spirit I wrote *The Frankenstein Dilemma*, the book you mentioned that provoked you to do this work. It was a strategy on my part—if I exposed both my own ideas, to a point, but also the dilemma surrounding them, I hoped it would cause others to pull back from work like mine and leave these types of experiments only to me, and me alone. But I don't believe anyone who read it, reviewed it, or studied my most well-known work knew exactly how close I was to this achievement, like spinning in front of a sun just before you burn.

It took me many months of trials to perfect the technology in such a manner as to feel confident to implant a healthy embryo into a woman's uterine lining. I decided to start this experiment by using an animal as well, but given my own hubris at that time, no ordinary lab mouse would do. I had my contact ship over two female pygmy tarsiers, the smallest primates in the world, from my mother's Indonesia. I was enjoying the symbolism of having these two female creatures from my

---

26 Shelley, *Frankenstein*.

mother's homeland make a child together. They were soft and fuzzy, like small monkeys, but with pug-like eyes that seemed ready to pop out of their heads. Using a process called invitro gametogenesis, also known as IVG, I planned to use cells from the tarsier that would not carry the embryo but transform them into material that could be mistaken as sperm and egg that could then create the embryo that would be implanted into the tarsier that would carry the pup. It was tricky science, but I had no doubt I would be successful.

I was told from the employees I crossed paths with as I entered the office each morning or left very late at night that our southern summer was absolutely exquisite that year, the region having had a most curious change, which resulted in a lowered humidity and heat index. But, as for me, I didn't know anything about it as I became so fixated on the project at hand, working at all hours of the morning and night. I neglected all the letters my mother, Ezra, and Hana sent to me once they'd learned I was close by. I remembered that just as I was leaving Oxford, my mother had written to me to let me know my grandmother had died in her sleep, imploring me to come home for her memorial service, and in either case, entreating me to keep my mother in my thoughts now and again. I received the true message behind her request, to remember her and my loved ones in my desperate obsession with my ambition. But I was unable to tear my eyes away from what I imagined would be worth all the distance I had built between myself and all those I loved. Once they realized what I had achieved, the entire world would be indebted to me and my endeavors. I imagined all the riches that would be bestowed on me, that the ones I loved would never want for anything again.

The remaining seasons of the year passed in much the same manner as that summer—I had no time for such flights of fancy as observing the world change. In retrospect, it was the uncontrollable quality of the changes in nature that I should have been more attentive to, as they may have led me to understand what I didn't see before it was too late. My cheeks grew sallow, and my body became thinner and thinner as I sacrificed food and wellness in order to reach the end of my quest. There were times I experienced brief moments of self-consciousness and reflection regarding how I must appear to others, not unlike the day you and your supervisor found me in my harried and unreasonable state. But I did not think much of it beyond a moment or two, and promptly I wormholed my way back to my pursuit, which was all that had the power to matter to me.

李

I knew it would take Ko some convincing, but I hoped love would be enough. Scratch that. I hoped the cost of my absence was enough. Of course, floating in my mind in the periphery was Ma, all the questions I asked myself to uncover why she left. But truthfully, the questions never involved her. They always circled back to me, as though I had the power in my small child body to loom that large. I asked if I bored her. I asked if I misbehaved too often. I asked if I wasn't white enough. I asked if my face wasn't sweet enough to miss when it wasn't in front of her. I asked if I was too much.

I suppose the worst part of it is that there is never a satisfying answer.

One night, Ko and I met at the park. Our usual. We emptied our canvas totes filled with sandwich Ziploc bags stuffed with granola bars and crackers, old plastic grocery bags weighed down with Capri Sun pouches and packets of trail mix. Ko leaned our loot against our favorite weeping willow, the one we always whispered to—the closest we ever got to prayer. *Please let us always love each other. Please let our parents never discover us. Please keep our secret from those who would tear us apart.* And then, the one I never said aloud: *Please make her stay.*

I grabbed Ko's hand and walked her to our favorite dirty park bench, its red paint faded and chipping on the bottom from overuse while the forest-dwellers crept their arms around the body of the tree from behind to grab the bags of snacks, then scampered away like the animals they slept with.

"Ko, I have to talk to you about something," I said softly that night, afraid, my eyes shifting to the stars overhead.

She briefly freed her hand from mine to touch my cheek, then brought it back.

"Plum? You okay?" Ko peered into my eyes, her own a pair of delicate question marks. She could see that something was up.

I gingerly grabbed a section of her long, dark hair, as dark as mine, and twisted it around my finger nervously. She loosened her hair from my finger, and grabbed my hands.

"Hey, just talk to me, okay? What's going on?"

"I just. I can't do it anymore. I can't stay there one more minute. I won't make it. Will you come with me?" I retrieved one of my hands to run my fingers nervously through my short hair, rubbed the back of my neck while I waited for her response.

Ko looked up to the sky I kept staring through, thinking. I tried to remember to breathe in and out, in and out. She sucked air through her teeth. I tried not to jump to conclusions about the space between my plea and her response. Tried to explain it to my heart as it bounced everywhere but in my chest.

"Woah, that's a lot. Damn. I know he's difficult but . . . where will we go? You sure you've thought this through?"

"I have. I'm just. I'm running out of options." My eyes shifted from left to right and everywhere in between. Ko touched my face again, and my eyes re-centered back on hers. "I totally get it, by the way, if you can't. But the anxiety of it all is killing me. I mean, I keep thinking, if he ever found out about us, I just, I don't know what he's—" My voice broke then into a mixture of weeping and incomprehensible speech. I didn't know what I'd survive less—staying with Ba or Ko gone from my life forever. Both felt inconceivable, but in wholly different ways.

"It's okay, it's okay, shhhhh." Ko stroked my head for several minutes, trying her best to soothe me, but she knew, partly, how useless it was. That it was Ba, that it was this, that there was no recovering from what he would make of my secret.

I gathered myself before I spoke again.

"I mean, we could stay here or at a shelter. We could get jobs and rent a room and maybe an apartment and then who knows? Queers have done this going back years and years and years. I know I'll be okay as long as you're with me. As long as I'm away from him. He lost it the other night when I was out with you. Of course, he didn't know what I was actually up to, but I could feel his suspicion boring into my skull. I just feel like the longer we sneak around, the harder it's gonna be to keep him from figuring it out. I just don't know what the fuck he'd do. I'm honestly petrified he'll just snap. I don't want to be on the other side of that, you know? Please?" I begged her, which was a bit humiliating, but I was desperate. I didn't know if I could go through with it on my own. I needed Ko. After my mother left, it was terrifying to need anyone.

I couldn't conceive of what Ba would do. I was too afraid to imagine it. But I couldn't go out into the world without Ko, either. It took some convincing, but by the time Ko and I parted that night, we had agreed we'd both leave home the same night, in two weeks, and meet back up at our bench. When I went to bed that night, I crossed all my fingers and toes like a child, hoping she wasn't just saying what I wanted to hear, but that she meant it. I felt silly, but hope was all I had to push forward.

Z

Before I tell you of the true catalyst that led to my tale of woe and ruin, I must first start by telling you a different story, one even I could not expect in my wildest nightmares. By the end of that summer, I had finally perfected the creature that would change not only the course of my life, but the future of all human life. Now that I had successfully created my little tarsier pups, I sold the ones that survived (that is, those that hadn't been cannibalized by the parents, as so often happens), as well as their parents on the black market to Indonesians who spent a pricey penny to keep them as designer pets. I planned to use the money I made for more research or maybe even my own separated lab for a new IVG clinic. I could already see my work would be heavily sought after once I managed to successfully create a human using the same means and could announce I'd made the perfect human species.

My species would have eyes of the clearest blue, just like my father's that had transfixed my mother so deeply so many years ago. I imagined this creature would have the masculine stature and musculature of the most admired athlete, the smoothest complexion that merged together the bronze coloring of my mother and the pale tones of the paperwhites that held so much power and influence in the world. Now that everything was in place, I planned to reunite with Hana. Although I imagined she would be hesitant at first, I would convince her to trust that we would make, together, the perfect children to reflect all of our best qualities. But there was an added variable we could not have ever seen coming.

While I was so fixated on my research at Oxford, Ezra had pursued his own journey. I had hoped, given my father's death, Ezra might return to those pursuits that had previously brought him so much joy. But it was too late. However, on the other hand, it did not seem as though Ezra had returned to my father's line of work either, which gave me some small comfort, as I assumed it meant he had let go of my father's deathbed mandate that we marry. At some point during my reclusive days of endless research, Ezra sent a letter saying that, among other trivialities, seeing how my work had brought me such focus and distraction from our father's death, he had also decided to study the reproductive sciences. Just as I had on that day with Hana so many moons ago, I became enraged at the idea Ezra would shadow me. I could only assume that he, too, intended to thwart the progress I was trying to make as a woman scientist.

After a long night in the lab, I retrieved Ezra's letter again from my nightstand where I had tossed it a few days prior and shredded it with my bare hands like an animal, promptly ridding my house of the evidence. Now that the letter no longer existed in the world, I banished it from my mind, convinced he would never conquer all the gains I had made since I last saw him. Since I hadn't heard a word of him from my fellow colleagues and the other prominent scientists in my field, I decided I had overreacted. Perhaps Ezra was trying to provoke me by antagonizing my known territorial nature. I returned to my work.

Even though it angered me that Ezra would even attempt to take what was mine, I was much too involved in my own research to give it attention for too long. Besides, we were so far apart from one another at this point, what harm could it do? Certainly, he would not be able to compete with me. I had been at this work my entire life, and he had been pursuing this new line of work for what, a year, two at best? I suppose, my ego being what it was, there was a tiny part of me that arose when the anxious part of me dissipated, one that took it as praise he was seeing my life as a model from which to find direction. But I would realize much too late Ezra's mirroring was only further evidence of the fact that Ezra still had not let go of the vow our father demanded we make to each other. I would learn later it was Ezra's belief that if he followed my intellectual pursuit, then maybe I would be more inclined to join him in this wedding pact. Although he had known about Hana so many years ago, provoking my father to burn all of the calalai clothes from my beloved trunk, I believe Ezra assumed Hana was long gone from my life, and that I was much too obsessed with my work to have found a new companion. Just as I pushed away all I loved to discover the secret behind creating life, so too did Ezra refuse to reflect upon any obstacle that could get in the way of fulfilling his father's deathbed promise.

I did not think further about this at the time. Ezra simply was of no great concern to me. No one was, truly. All that mattered to me was my work. No one mattered when I was so singularly occupied with creating a being that would no longer require the need of men.

In retrospect, I should have thought more about what his mirroring of my own inquiries might have meant for my future in this realm. But, whatever the case, he wrote to me again, informing me he would be in town, and asked to come visit the lab. *Perhaps we could have a long overdue reunion*, he signed off sweetly. He had heard great things about my prestigious facilities, he wrote in the letter, and it was these words of praise and validation I found myself charmed by enough to allow Ezra to briefly pause my work. Ezra also suggested that, if I found his portfolio to my liking, that perhaps my lab might find a suitable position for him. As he started to come closer and closer to orbiting my own universe, the disconcerted feeling I had over him encroaching upon a territory I had long claimed as my own began to grow more intensely; but nonetheless, I naively imagined I could take one evening out of my work to share a simple dinner with him, politely decline his request for a job, and that would be the end of it. Of course, I thought to myself, I would generously offer him a reference, and to that end, I brought with me a list of the top embryology labs in the country, stored safely out of sight in my briefcase, one almost identical to the one I had borrowed from my father that day long ago: Deep brown leather with gold locks. I was certain that, in the end, he would seek out a lab far from mine. I wish I had realized that it was never the career he was after. Only me.

When the receptionist brought Ezra to my office, it was hard not to think about the many years I had known Ezra throughout my life and how different Ezra appeared to me from the young, sweet cherubic child I still envisioned in my mind. His golden curls had been gone for many years now, and the bright yellow of his locks had been replaced by a dark brown that reminded me of the chocolate candies he used to buy at the market for five cents and pop into his mouth before our mother saw him. Perfectly coiffed, Ezra kept the slightest hint of a bouffant just above his forehead, while the rest of his hair was shaved quite close to the back of the neck and sides of his head. When we stood to greet one another, I was stunned at how tall he had become. His frame, long and lean like a beanpole, was eerily similar to our father's. The soft delicate nature I had so long associated with my Ezra had been replaced with a rigid, confident air, one I wish I had questioned more at the time.

"Sister, Cousin, darling, how are you?" Ezra joked as he greeted me, referencing the many roles we had performed for each other since we were young children. This new Ezra was a stranger, unrecognizable from the young boy I grew up with.

He offered me each cheek to kiss. I brusquely offered him my hand instead. Ezra smirked at me and took it.

I was wearing a three-piece pinstripe suit, two-toned knot cufflinks that were silver and blue, and men's brown leather oxfords to match my briefcase. As I shook Ezra's hand, I motioned for my receptionist, Leonard, to be excused.

"Leonard, please bring my car around front and make sure to lock up when you leave for the day. This is my brother, Ezra, and we'll be having dinner down the street. I'll return to work afterwards." I readjusted my cuff at my wrist, lightly fingering my cufflink.

"Yes, Dr. Frank," Leonard replied with a deferential nod, shutting the door behind him. Ezra observed the exchange between us, the fact that my receptionist referred to me by Dr. Frank rather than our given surname, without saying a word.

Our dinner was fairly harmless. We chatted about our different paths towards similar scientific goals since we'd last seen one another. Ezra told me he had decided to leave our father's business behind and how he came to be interested in IVF, but the story felt forced and flat. But mostly, he wanted to spend our time together sharing memories about our father, not work. I made it clear that this was not a topic of interest to me. It seemed to catch him a bit off guard, but he adapted quickly enough, and we moved onto other superficial topics of conversation. Nevertheless, the dinner was relatively innocuous, as I had anticipated. I felt some small whirring of anxiety beneath the skin, but I convinced myself it was only due to how strange and unfamiliar this man, whom I once felt closer to than our mother, seemed.

It was when I began to walk Ezra to his car at the lab that

the nightmare began.

I began to rifle through my briefcase for the list of labs he could contact for employment. "I'm sorry we don't have any openings right now, Ezra"—I continued rummaging through the briefcase for the printouts—"but here is a list of the top labs in the country. I would be happy to write you a letter of reference if you find yourself interested in a position at one of them."

"Sister," he said, placing his fingers around my wrist. We were standing in front of his car. "I don't need your pity, or your charity." I looked down at his hand holding my wrist and back up at his face to ascertain if this touch was aggressive or gentle.

"Could you please let go?" I asked, quickly scanning the parking lot to confirm we were alone and many feet from anyone that would see or hear us. The dark was menacing. I knew the power a man held in his fingertips. I had seen my father with my mother. I knew it wouldn't take much for Ezra to hurt me. No one would stop him.

He gripped my wrist tighter.

"Ezra, I am asking you to stop," I said, this time more forcefully than the last.

Ezra leaned forward to give me an unwanted kiss on my lips. I turned my face to shrug him off, but before I could, he cornered me next to the driver's door of his car, pushy and hostile in a manner I had never before witnessed from him. I had not known Ezra as a man. He pinned my shoulders against the cold metal of the door with one arm. With the other arm he grabbed a ring box out of his coat pocket, opening it with his free thumb. Inside the velvet ring box was an extravagant diamond ring.

"This is not up for debate, Zoelle," he said. Hearing that old name again, a name I had not used for many years, made me nauseous. It was hard to speak. So I remained silent.

"In order for our father to have eternal peace, he insisted we wed. I hope you will understand why we must do this. After we marry, I plan to take control of your lab. Oil is a bit unpredictable for my tastes, so I'm sure Father would agree that letting the business go was the best thing I could have done for the family." Ezra took the ring out of the box and began to lift my hand. I took advantage of the temporary distraction and kicked him in the ankle.

"You will never get my lab. I will never marry you," I said. Although my entire body pulsated with rage and fear, I remained calm from an innate need to survive this man in front of me who was no longer my brother, cousin, or anyone I would call a tender heart, like I had so many years ago.

Ezra grabbed his ankle and started rubbing it vigorously, cursing at me. At that moment, a car pulled up next to us, their headlights blaring, the window rolled down.

"Hey, you okay?" a young woman asked.

"Oh yes, madam, there's no need to worry. We're fam—" Ezra began, but by then I had slipped into the woman's car and asked her to drive me to the garage. The next day, I went to Leonard and told him to tell the security detail in the lab that Ezra was to have no access to any part of the lab, in case he claimed he had my permission. I wouldn't find out for some time that my warnings wouldn't prevent Ezra from acting however he wished.

It took me two weeks to recover from Ezra's visit. I couldn't work. I couldn't sleep. I spent many nights in the lab, my eyes peeled for the tiniest shift in atmosphere, the slightest hint of a noise that would alert me Ezra had returned to lay claim to the only thing I had built with my own two hands. Ezra wasn't even my blood relative. How could he stake claim over something he didn't even inherit? Come to think of it, I don't even know if my father ever legally adopted him from the orphanage. If he could have gotten away with it, he would have just grabbed him from that patch of grass that one bright morning in Norway. The orphanage would have had no idea where to even look for this little cherubic toddler who was playing outside one moment and gone the next. Although Ezra had come into our lives suddenly, perhaps it had never been sudden for my father. Perhaps this adoption had been in the works for some time, kept a secret from even my mother.

All I knew was this: I had worked way too hard and for far too long to let this miniaturized version of my father take what had always been mine.

But, as each day passed into the next and I did not see any sign of Ezra, my pulse began to recede, and I proceeded with my project to create new life in ways we had only dreamed of.

It was time to bring Hana into this universe that I had traveled in isolated and alone, that had long been the reason for my disappearance. On one of the first days I felt secure enough to sleep in my own home, I made my way to my nightstand, where a stack of unopened letters from Hana sat. I grabbed the one with the most recent postmark and without opening it, I copied the return address from her envelope onto my own. I took out a piece of paper and began to write.

My dearest Hana,

I am so deeply sorry for how absent I've been to you these many months. I hope, if you accept my invitation, that you will forgive me once you learn what I've been doing all of this time. I can't wait to show you what I have been up to lately. Please come to me. I have much news for you, news I believe will bring you much happiness. At least, that is my wish. Enclosed is a ticket by plane, train, and bus, one way, to where I live and work. Please come as soon as you can. I need you.

Yours, Z.

Two weeks later, Hana arrived at the lab by the car service I had arranged for her.

She was still as luminous and elegant as I had remembered her, but I now saw fatigue etched into the lines of her face and her deep-set eyes that had not been there before. It saddened me, but I didn't mention a word of my observations. All that mattered to me in that moment, in any moment, was the task at hand that I hoped Hana would help me bring to fruition.

Much to her boredom and disinterest, I began relaying to

her the scientific technicalities of the discoveries I had made since we'd last seen one another.

"Hana, remember that fight we had—our first fight—when we were eating on our blanket by the willow?" I nudged her. She smiled. "I couldn't possibly forget how I found all that exciting research for you and you shredded it into little bits!" Hana's thick curls fell around each side of her face as she laughed.

"I know, I know," I said, laughing along with her. "How absolutely terrible I was then." I looked downward in mock guilt. "But, look. Now, I have discovered that what you found that one day all those years ago has led me to my greatest work." I grabbed her hand, the first time we touched in so many moons, and lifted her chin up with my free hand so that her eyes met mine. "This is something we can do now, together."

Hana looked at me with openness, a hint of confusion.

"Here, love. Let me show you."

Continuing to hold her hand, I guided her into the restricted lab, so that she could see the egg I had made with my own blood and skin.

"This is an egg I made of my own cells. The beginning of our child, of all that we could ever want for our future. We don't even need a real egg or sperm to do it. Take a look." My voice began to accelerate, turning wild in my throat. I couldn't help it. It was the moment I had been waiting for my entire life. All I needed was for Hana to say yes. I stood behind her as she looked into the microscope, which I had adjusted so that she could see the egg clearly.

"Wow. Z, that's incredible! But what about sperm?" Hana ventured carefully, her hand reaching back to touch my shoulder as she looked at the me in the dish below.

"Don't you see?" I grabbed her by both shoulders and turned her around to face me. She took a step back, and I tried to reel in my excitement. "We can do the same thing! I was thinking, what if the sperm could be used with the same process but from you? Then our child truly could be ours together, just like a traditional man and woman's can be." My breath grew rapid and hot, burning my chest and throat as it poured out of me.

Hana chewed on her lip and didn't say a word.

"Do you mind if I take a few minutes to take a walk through the building to think through all of this? I just—" she began to respond, but I interrupted her.

"Don't even give it a second thought. Please," I said, gesturing towards the door. "Take all the time you need." I attempted to feign patience, but my body tingled with urgency.

I lost track of how long she was gone from the lab. Just as I was starting to lose all confidence that she would join me on this magnificent quest, I heard her soft fist knock on the secured door to the room that contained the egg I had created from my own matter.

When I opened the door, Hana fell into my arms. She scattered a hundred little kisses across my face, like the touch of little flying things. "Let's start a life together," she whispered into my ears. I sighed rapturously, but Hana's rapture and mine were altogether very distinguished from one another.

"You mean it?" I asked, breathless, my face flushed from her touch.

"Yes, love. I would love nothing more than for us to finally start our life together. But," she paused, biting her lip.

"Yes, darling, what is it?" I grew anxious again.

"I need you to understand that my work is important for me, too. Once the baby is born, I will want to focus on my own career. I can't wait to tell you more about it." In one of the letters, I had read that she was pursuing a doctorate in gender studies, but I assumed once she felt the excitement of this far superior work, she would abandon her path that was the path of so many.

"Oh, but of course! And I want you to tell me everything," I assured her, taking her into my arms and kissing her.

"But who will carry it?" she asked after we came up for air.

"Oh, yes, we should talk about that," I started, clearing my throat.

"I was hoping that you would be willing to carry the child. Since this will be my first experiment of this nature, I want to take copious notes on how the fetus develops in utero. It would just be easier if I wasn't being impacted by the effects of pregnancy," I said.

"Your first," she paused. "Experiment."

"You know what I mean, darling!" I held her in my arms. "I mean, it will be the start of our future. But it will also be the beginning of my work, too. You understand, don't you?"

I moved my head back from where it rested on her shoulder to scan her face for agreement. Her stoic expression gradually grew into a grin.

"Well, as the femme, I always assumed I would carry our child. I think pregnancy is such a magical opportunity not everybody has the privilege to experience," she admitted, grinning.

"I didn't dare assume, but the idea of pregnancy, of having one's condition so externalized on your physical form has never quite appealed to me, to be frank," I smirked.

"That reminds me. You call yourself Dr. Frank these days?" she winked.

"Yes. It suits me. I call myself Z for short."

"Z Frank. I like it," she said, nuzzling her nose into my neck.

*

After weeks of painstaking labor and calculation, I was able to create viable sperm cells from Hana's blood and skin. We were elated when the day came to fertilize the egg into an embryo we would implant into Hana's uterus. However, our exciting mission would be thwarted, and we would not learn until too late how disastrously.

I would learn something was amiss on the day that I planned to fertilize the egg. When I opened the secret lab which held my egg, I noticed something strange and terrifying. The egg was no longer, and there, in its place, was a fully fertilized embryo. Hana's sperm remained in its place, intact. No one was allowed in that room. No one. I panicked. I fled the room and ran to my office, immediately summoning Leonard.

"Dr. Frank, how can I assist?" Leonard asked, standing close to the door. I held my hands in my lap underneath the desk, trying as hard as I could to hold them tight enough to prevent them from tremoring.

"Is there anything you need to tell me?" I asked as calmly as possible.

"Oh. Well, we have had to switch out a few of the security personnel, for a number of various reasons I thought you needn't be burdened with while you work on your important study," he said.

"I see. Could you check to see if they let anyone that was unauthorized into the lab in the last five days?" I asked, my voice shallower than I had ever remembered hearing it.

"Certainly, Doctor. Is everything alright?"

"Just, please. Go ask them. As soon as possible." Without a word of response, Leonard excused himself.

I sat in my office with my eyes closed, rolling beneath their lids, my heart jolting in my chest. What would I tell Hana? It couldn't be possible, I reasoned with myself. There were so many layers of security one had to pass to enter that secret room. But how else could an egg have been fertilized? Who else would have been able to do this? And so quickly? As more questions ran feverishly through my mind, I was disrupted by a loud series of knocks on the door.

"Dr. Frank? It's me, Leonard. I have the information you are after."

"Please, come in."

Leonard entered with a young man I had never seen before, dressed in civilian clothes, his head hanging low. That is when I knew what had happened.

"Dr. Frank, this is Preston. I am afraid he has very distressing news. As you can see, he will no longer be welcome on the premises. Go ahead, Preston. Tell Dr. Frank what you told me. Dr. Frank, you and I can change the passcode after I complete his exit interview."

Preston told me that an incredibly well-dressed and well-mannered young man insisted that he was my brother and that I had given him permission to access the lab so that he could assist me with my current work. Of course, it did not occur to Preston to be suspicious of a man who claimed to be my family. The secret room required a special passcode to enter, and since I never foresaw myself in a situation where I would have to protect my property from Ezra, I did not think twice about using calalai as my secret passcode. Who, in the middle of the American South, would ever know this word, this Indonesian name, for what I was? So few people even considered this possibility when they saw me in my suits and ties, my treasured briefcase. I had never uttered this word aloud to a single person besides my mother and Hana. But Ezra had his ways.

The damage was done. I had come so far. I couldn't stop now. I couldn't let Ezra's act of sabotage undo all the years of sacrificing sleep, food, and all other comforts, in order to see this work through to fruition. I would not let a man stop me now.

So, I made a decision. One that would forever alter the

course of my life, Hana's life, the lives of so many others. I chose to proceed as planned, and I withheld the truth from Hana about the embryo. That the embryo did not contain Hana's genetic material, but mine and Ezra's.

A few days later, the embryo I had painstakingly created after many months of work was successfully transferred into Hana's uterus. We were elated to verify by ultrasound a few weeks later that my experiment was successful. Hana was pregnant. However, our delight was short lived.

There were occasions during Hana's pregnancy in which I worried about the fallout of Ezra's actions. I didn't know where he had trained or how well he knew the techniques of IVG. It was not until after the first trimester I learned what had happened as a consequence of Ezra's actions and my refusal to wait. Since we were already in uncharted territory, we had no idea what kind of mutations this might ultimately cause the fetus I had worked so tirelessly to create without egg or sperm. But it was during an ultrasound after the first trimester that I deduced Ezra and I were both carriers for a genetic mutation associated with gigantism and acromegaly.

Hana's belly was already beginning to stretch the fabric of her oversized T-shirt. Fatigue and confusion crowded her thoughts more and more each day, but even in her state, she could tell I was keeping something from her.

"Z? What is it? Is something wrong with the baby?" she asked, her face lined with worry. I sat next to her and laid my head against her belly while she stroked my hair.

"Tell me, Z. What is it? Whatever it is, we have to work

this out together." I started to cry. Hana repositioned herself so that she was sitting upright. I lifted my head to face her.

"Z. Whatever is happening to my body. I need you to tell me what's going on. Now." She spoke with an insistence I had never heard from her before. It startled me.

"I don't even know how to begin to tell you this. But." I paused. Hana uncharacteristically ran her fingers through her hair.

"The day I planned to use your sperm to fertilize my egg. Well. I discovered that the egg had already been fertilized. It was already an embryo." I took a deep breath.

"What? By who? Whose sperm is inside me, Z?" Hana clutched her belly, and I couldn't tell if she was protecting it from the world, or from me.

"Ezra had coerced his way into the lab. It's Ezra's sperm. I didn't tell you because I was hoping everything would turn out in the end and that this would be the first of many children we would have. But. It looks like both Ezra and I are carriers for a genetic mutation that may be linked to gigantism."

"I cannot believe you would do this. I cannot believe you would care about your precious work over my life. Over our child. You could have just started the process over. But you never listen. You are always so impatient, so self-obsessed, to be the idol. At all costs." A single tear froze on Hana's cheek, but it was one of rage, an emotion I always associated with myself but never with her.

She rushed out of the room.

Hana did not come home for many nights. All kinds of

dreadful thoughts ran through my mind, mostly about what would happen to my work now that the woman carrying the child that bore my life's work was gone, now that the child that held what mattered could end in a miscarriage, or a stillbirth, or even worse. I tried to banish the worst-case scenarios from my mind.

After several days, Hana returned to me while I was at home, different than she was before. Composed. The temperament of ice.

"I have some things to say," Hana said, sitting with me at the small wooden dining table where she had found me. I reached for her hand, but she kept hers in her lap, underneath the table. I retrieved mine after a moment and did the same.

"It is too late to have an abortion, now that the state has imposed tighter restrictions on late-term abortions. I suppose we could travel out of state or even fly to Canada, but it's too risky. Because of the special circumstances under which this child was created, you are the only person that can most safely bring this child into the world. Since you did not give me all the information to make a sound decision about what was to happen inside my own body, I am now having this child against my will. I am nothing more than an empty vessel to you, a container to hold your secrets and your ambitions. I see that now, even though it is far too late for me to do anything about it." Hana took a drink from a glass of water in front of her. I started to respond, but she silenced me with one hand.

"I will see this through. I have no choice that won't also endanger my life as well. But after I have this experiment, as you so aptly called it, I will wash my hands of it. And of you." She grabbed her glass of water from the table and walked into the second bedroom and did not emerge from her room for the rest of the night.

Hana did not speak to me for weeks after discovering what Ezra had done, and what I had let continue without a word. At first, I gave her the distance she clearly desired, but I grew weary of it after some time and threw many fits, hoping to convince her to speak to me again. I missed her warmth and her openness, her kisses, and her embrace. I didn't exactly blame her, for it was true that she was now being forced to carry a child against her will largely so that I could work out my ideas on her body. Her one opportunity to have the child be part hers squandered by my own brother. And to make matters worse, now this child would possibly be born with a genetic disorder that would even ruin the entire purpose of its conception. We did not know what would come of this creation now that it had been tampered with by the very source we had attempted to relinquish in our process. Even with all of this, I did not hold myself fully accountable for what happened to Hana. It was too easy to blame Ezra for all of my woes and for Hana's spurning of me. Hana continued onwards with her pregnancy, as she had no other option, and our relationship became that of two colleagues watching a vine grow out of a mound of dirt.

There was only one thing left to do now. Wait.

李

The night I left, Ba was still finishing his hospital rounds. He wouldn't be home for hours. I left a note pinned to his pillowcase—vague enough he wouldn't be completely caught off guard, but not clear enough for him to know the real reason I left. I packed a small duffel with what I couldn't bear to live without, and then I called a car to take me to meet Ko at our spot.

To tell you the truth, I didn't fully expect her to be there when the car dropped me off. Why would she? No one in my life up until then had proved to me anything otherwise. But I still hoped she would be the one to stay.

But she was. She was there.

I couldn't help it. At first, I let myself believe in some kind of permanence. When we first left home, we had the hardest time finding somewhere to rest our heads. And so, we started to become like the ones we used to forage for, transient woodland creatures subsisting on berries hanging from trees and food left in garbage cans or by kind strangers. Like the ones we used to be.

We were cut off from the world, Ko and I, but on that account we became very attached to one another.[27] I hoped with everything in me that we would always be together.

But within her, Ko held onto a different hope—that her parents could change, that they would accept her as she was. She didn't look like me, so I imagine it was different for her—her beautiful milky skin, her long hair, her feminine way of navigating the world. She could hide the secret more easily. I wasn't so lucky. I couldn't hide what I was or who I loved from anyone. Outside of Ba, I had no desire to.

Although we occasionally found warm rooms with beds at the local shelter, Ko found it more difficult to equate herself with the other queer runaways, the transient souls who couldn't make their way through their dependence on MDMA or alcohol. I didn't mind it so much—I felt less alone knowing there were others in the world like me who didn't feel rooted anywhere. I had never felt a pull towards anything that would alter my perception of the world. That felt too scary. But Ko's story wasn't like mine. She had parents who couldn't understand her, but they didn't have a fierce hand like Ba, or an inability to stay, like Ma. I know now she never wanted to be like the woodland creatures generous enough to share their tiny blanket with us or stretch their small findings of food to accommodate three

27 Shelley, *Frankenstein.*

instead of one. I'll always remember that she tried just because she loved me.

It was a cold night when Ko told me she was going back.

We were lying under a worn blanket someone had abandoned in a dumpster, trying to keep each other warm with it and our body heat. We could have built a fire, but a fire would have made us more visible, perhaps risking our arrest. Then we would have been back to square one.

"Plum?" Her two soft feet sandwiched mine from where she held me from behind, a move she would instantly make when we slept. It's the reason I called her Koala, aka Ko. Ko's cheek rested against the dip between my shoulder blades. She took back her arm that was holding my belly to tug on my earlobe with her hand.

"Koko? What is it?"

She pushed my shoulder down so that I would turn my body around to face her.

"I'm going back. Plum, I'm so sorry. I can't do it. I wish I could, but I'm not like you. I'm not so strong, I just—" Her words dissolved into tears. I held her like she had held me so many times before.

"Shhhhh. It's not about strength. It's just the only way I can survive. But I understand," I whispered into her ear, not wanting anyone around us to hear. "Hey, look at me," I said softly, raising her face to meet mine. Her face was beautiful and held such depth, even in the dark, even at this moment when I knew I would soon never see her again. "It will always mean so much to me that you tried. More than I can ever tell you," I said to her, tears filling my eyes.

We spent the rest of the night holding each other, our tears wetting the backs of each other's shirts. By noon the following day, Ko was gone.

When Ko said she was going back, we knew what it meant. That I couldn't. But I suppose if I'm being honest with myself, I always knew that she would never be able to sustain this life of transience. If she hadn't left, maybe I never would have found my way to Dr. Frank's lab. A social worker named Marjorie helped me get my GED, which gradually led me to college on a full scholarship, and then to graduate school, and finally, to trying to help others build their families. I wanted to give others what I always craved for myself. If I couldn't have a family, at least I could help others manifest it for themselves with fortunate access to new technologies. If they could afford it.

After life on the streets and losing my Ko, my heart, sculpture seemed the most trivial pursuit in the world. I couldn't imagine a time that life would be that simple ever again. Besides, sculpture reminded me too much of Ko now. It was too painful to go back to that life. Ko became another tender bird in my hand like Ma—due to how overwhelming I was, she got away from me. It hurt too much to make things, to remember Ko's hands behind me helping me mold the plaster or clay into something better than I could envision, her hair falling over my shoulder.

The only way forward was through, and the only way through was to envision a rebirth, shedding the life I once had and starting anew. It was better to move on and hope I could, in some way, help others find their Kos, their Mas, their little creatures of joy.

Z

Hana gave birth at the beginning of the following summer. I'd like to say we were met with the joy and delightful anticipation I had offered so many couples in our position. But our moment of rapture and love was stillborn.

Because we had no idea what this child would mutate into, during her pregnancy, Hana read obsessively about gigantism and acromegaly until I pried the books from her hands after she had fallen asleep, the only time I would venture to touch her again. At times I heard her on the phone, whispering, but the minute she heard my footsteps pass near the spare room, she'd stop speaking. She must have been sharing something with someone—her parents?—about what I had done that she did not want me to overhear. She continued to sleep in the spare room throughout the duration of the pregnancy, stacks of books on doulas, home births, and general guides on IVG, IVF and rare genetic disorders on the two nightstands on each side of the small bed where she slept. She never left that room. I believe it was so she could hide herself from me and our creation from the world, since we had no idea whether this creation would be fit for society. I often wondered what attachment, if any, she was forming with the creature building inside of her. We barely spoke more than a few words to one another.

She continued to let me examine her for her routine checkups, and she asked after the development of the child following each appointment. We hired a queer Black midwife, Silber, who Hana found on her own without consulting me. She trusted in Silber to keep the circumstances of this unique birth confidential and her skills to aid us in whatever complications might arise. I greatly grieved Hana's touch and attention, but I was far too occupied with my own fears as to how this child I had spent my life's work building would turn out. All of that effort only for Ezra to ruin everything I had built.

For the most part, all of the ultrasounds I performed on Hana leading up to the birth did not depict anything out of the ordinary, although her belly was already protruding in ways that seemed surprising for her petite frame. Early in the pregnancy, it looked as though Hana might even have twins, which brought me great excitement, for I hoped it would mean that if one egg were to have the genetic mutation, perhaps the other would be saved. But later on, we would learn that one egg had vanished, consumed by the other. Those eggs felt, in some way, like Ezra and me. I thought we would always be each other's darlings, but it seemed we were in a fight to the death, one our father had started but that would continue long after he had died. Who would win? The size of the creature inside Hana's belly gradually became a concern to us both, one we had negotiated on our own and separate spheres since I discovered the possibility of a genetic disorder. Hana was already so big even a full month before her due date that after careful consideration, I brought in Silber for her urgent guidance.

Silber was in her midforties. Because we called her so late into the pregnancy, she came to the door that day dressed for anything. Her usual bright silk fabrics were replaced with a set of functional scrubs, her hair kept out of her face with a simple black headwrap. She brought a simple canvas tote bag with her, slung across one shoulder, and without so much as offering a greeting, she ran into Hana's room.

"Silber, thank god you're here," Hana screamed out to her, with one hand clutching her belly, the other reaching out for Silber, who swiftly ran to her side.

"Darling, how are you? I hear you're quite full and still a month to go. Let me have a look," Silber said, measured and calm. Pressing a firm hand on various parts of Hana's belly, Silber asked Hana to breathe into her hand again and again, giving her nods of encouragement as she examined her.

"Good, that's good. Now, let me just listen to your heart, take your pulse, and your blood pressure," she said, going into her bag and grabbing her stethoscope and her blood pressure monitor.

She didn't say a word for several minutes.

"Z? Where are you?" she called out to me. I ran into Hana's room from the kitchen where I had been pacing, trying to give both of them space and privacy during the examination.

"I'm here, I'm here. How's the baby?" I looked at Hana, who looked away from me, towards the window. Silber took out a vial of soap and a pair of gloves.

"That baby needs to get out. I'm not sure how it's grown so large already, but Hana said there might be some sort of genetic defect?"

"Not defect!" I said brusquely, without realizing my tone. Silber raised one eyebrow at me.

"Sorry. No, not defect. A possible genetic mutation that could result in a disorder. Of gigantism."

"Ah, okay. I wish you would have given me this information sooner. Hana assumed you had already advised me. Very well then. I think we have no choice but to induce. Now. I will do my best to do this on my own, but it is possible, given the nature of the baby's condition, that she will need a hospital," she said, walking over to the bathroom sink and carefully washing her hands. She then fitted each glove over her hands.

Hana screamed out in protest. Silber walked back over to her, holding her hand.

"I'm sorry, darling. I really will do the best I can to bring this baby into the world as safely as I can. You have my promise. We will do what we can, but there is still a chance you will need hospital care, okay? But let's see what we can do first." Silber touched Hana's face. I was struck with a pang of jealousy, but I willed it to pass. Hana nodded.

How can I describe what a catastrophe this pinnacle moment, this moment I had been waiting my entire life for, became? The creature's head was too large and unwieldy to fit through the birth canal, and Hana was under major duress and pain. We had no choice but to rush Hana to the hospital for an emergency C-section. When we got to the hospital, I could tell by the look on the admitting doctor's face that this was not something he dealt with on a regular basis. It was at that moment that Hana finally looked back at me. We shared a silent glance, a shared feeling of tremendous fright, for we knew that the genetic mutation of this child was not altogether unexpected. Now that we were certain it was here, there was no denying it.

But then came the release of blood that was the result of this distorted creature and the responsibility of that boy, little Ezra, who had for so many years brought so much charm and joy into my life. Sweat began to pour from the top of Hana's head during the procedure, and the doctor struggled furiously to pull the enormous being out of Hana's swollen belly while Silber remained by Hana's side, stroking her hand and coaxing her through it. At times, the doctor would ask Silber to assist, but mostly, she just remained of support to Hana, for which I was grateful. Hana certainly had not warmed towards me, not even now, even when so much was at stake. I suppose, looking back, the more dangerous and painful the childbirth became, the colder she became towards me—the reason for its acceleration.

I had never seen so much blood in my life. It was a grotesque sight I hope to never revisit. Good god, what I thought would have been the most perfect specimen. The creature's eyes were indeed blue, as I had hoped, but there was an eerie hollowness to them, like staring into a dazzling crystallized light. Its complexion was an intriguing dark blonde color, but the amount of reddened hair sprouting from its head and belly was disconcerting to say the least. Its belly button protruded an inch from its body, and its rib cage caused its torso to stick so far out that I could only describe its manner as absolutely wretched. The infant's hands were abnormally large while its feet, shockingly, remained a more expected size.

The only comfort I had at this hideous sight was also a tragedy. Hana had lost so much blood during the C-section that she didn't survive through the procedure long enough to even see this monster the doctor placed in my hands before he fled the scene.

For so many years I had worked at nothing else other than my attempt at creating the perfect creature, one untouched by a man either in the creation of the embryo or in its delivery. In the end, I lost control over both of these variables. It was these factors that led to my poor creature's ruin and ugliness. In order to accomplish this, I had kept all whom I loved far from me, and I had sacrificed all sense of wellness and happiness. *But now that the creature was in front of me, the beauty of the dream vanished, and breathless horror and disgust filled my heart.*[28] Unable to endure the aspect of the being I had created, and over whose perfection I was unable to fully control, I took the infant, covered in a white sheet, into my arms and rushed out of the room.

---

28 Shelley, *Frankenstein.*

Because I had long held a certain kind of authority in the town, I was easily recognizable to most healthcare professionals. Most knew how important I was to the birth industry. As I walked the hallways of the hospital, I could see the shock held on the faces of the nurses and the hospital administrative staff who had clearly already been told what had transpired in that room between me, Hana, Silber, and the attending doctor. I emitted some sort of energy or held some reaction on my face indicating that whatever it was I held in my arms, shielded from view with a thin, white bed sheet, was so horrible and unseemly that no one asked after me or questioned why I was leaving without filling out the appropriate paperwork.

This was not a creature I wanted to claim. I did not want my name attached to any birth certificate for this bundle tucked under my arm. No social security number. No proper identification. This creature killed my love and was marked with the poison of my brother, my cousin, my darling Ezra who had become a stranger before my very eyes. Perhaps he had always been one. I would never see this thing our sick twisted triangle had made separate from Hana's gruesome death and Ezra's manipulation, the sole reason for this thing's monstrousness. This creation was coated in the sheen of tragedy and destruction, for now and all eternity. Everyone knew not to stop me or question what I hid between my hands. I'm sure they remained silent and unmoving in fear of what could be so terrible to be hidden from the world by its own creator.

As I raced out of the room, I heard Silber, who had silently remained with Hana, frozen in shock and grief at Hana's death, cry out after me, but I think she knew after what she had witnessed that there was no use catching me. We knew we would never see each other again. We would never speak of what we had experienced together in that sterile room. I hoped to never return to this place again. I didn't look back to see if she had run after me or if she remained glued to the chair by Hana's side.

I ran to a nearby forest. In a state of frenzy and confusion, I left the newborn at the base of a tree, telling myself I would return for it after I cleared my head. I would figure out what to do then. I returned to the hospital to tend to Hana's body. But I knew in my heart that nothing could bring me back to that tree, that hideous being, and the scene of the failure of my one dream and love.

After roaming the streets for several hours with no purpose or destination in mind other than to flee what I had witnessed and erase it from my mind, I finally exhausted myself and walked the long distance homeward, hoping it would help me sleep off this nightmare. A little part of me wished I would wake up to discover it had all been a most terrible dream. That Hana and the unborn baby were still with me. That she loved me again. That I had thrown away the embryo that contained Ezra's sperm and told her everything from the beginning, so we could just start again. Instead, as I slept, I was tormented by the most disturbing visions. I saw little Ezra, as he was from so long ago, when my father and grandmother were still alive, but it was as though his and my father's faces had merged into one, one pair of piercing eyes of blue. Having not seen my father in so long, I immediately went to embrace him without thinking, but as I pulled away to greet him properly, I discovered holes where his eyes should be, his flesh rotting off his bones.

I spent the rest of the night monstrously. For days afterward, I feared I would fall into an unconscious state from the agony I experienced then. My pulse sped; my eyes could not rest long on a subject of focus. I felt such striking grief at all that I had lost—Hana, little Ezra, but most of all, the bitter and disappointing distance between how I had imagined my creation and what demonic reality took its place instead.

At some point, I felt an indefinable remorse at leaving a defenseless infant in the woods with no sustenance or comfort, even one as hideous as that which I had made; and so, one night shortly after the creature's birth, I stole away from my apartment in the middle of the night. I imagine if anyone had come upon me, I would have looked dreadfully sallow and hysterical with a certain wildness in my eyes. By the time I reached the tree where I had set the baby in the white sheet from the hospital, the wretched thing was gone, the sheet wrapped around one of the tree's branches, making a whipping sound with the wind.

*

Although visions of the wretched being I had made fluttered into my consciousness from time to time, for the most part I spent the next many years trying to shut the horrid incident out of my mind completely. I continued on with my work. I kept my distance from my mother and Ezra, for there was no way I could forgive Ezra for what he had done, and I could imagine no way to explain to my mother all that had transpired between us. I didn't know if Ezra realized the extent of his destructive act of revenge. I had no idea what had become of him since his heinous act. I often wondered if he assumed I destroyed the embryo once I'd inevitably realized he had sabotaged my efforts. Did he ever wonder what became of his vile material? I assume, like most men, that he went about his life without giving a moment's attention to all he had destroyed or the life he might have created, except, perhaps, some self-satisfaction at having caused me pain in exchange for my refusal of his proposal. He knew he could never force me to marry him. Not here. Not like my father forced my mother to wed him so many years ago.

Those years following the birth were the darkest I had ever experienced. I no longer engaged with my employees or, for that matter, anyone. With Hana, I buried any chance at a future with another. How could I merge my life with anyone else's after what I allowed to happen to her? I killed her. Or rather, I allowed her to become collateral damage in the pursuit of creation and ambition. And for what? Why was Nature so cruel as to allow her to die and then leave me to live in agony? Life in those years was a torturous endeavor, and I aimed not to allow myself any joy or prospect of opportunity beyond the small moves forward I made with my lab. When others asked how my work was going, I said whatever I could to quell the conversation and be done with it. The truth was too painful to speak to anyone. I could barely admit it to myself.

It would take sixteen years before I uncovered what happened to the being I recklessly and foolishly created. Sixteen years to learn what became of the golden-haired child I loved so much. Sixteen years away from the soulless world I then inhabited. By that time, I had long banished the monster of my early years from my memory as best I could. I assumed the thing had not made it through infancy, given that it was, by my own hand, left out in the elements on the bare earth without nourishment, love, or protection.

It was on this day, sixteen years later, I would receive a most unwanted letter that changed the course of my life forever. After a particularly long night at the lab with the other specialists, I came home to find a letter from my mother waiting for me. Initially, I was surprised she would send me something by mail when certainly she could have called me on the phone or sent me an email. But given that I had removed myself from all interaction with the family—I never told her why I stopped coming to visit during the holidays, and she respected my choice by not inquiring further—it may have been the only option she felt she had at her disposal. An unexpected letter from her certainly injected my veins with anxiety. I immediately wondered if something terrible had happened. Whatever I imagined, however, was not remotely close to what the contents of the letter revealed.

My Dearest Zoelle—

I hope this letter finds you well. It has been so many years since I have seen your face. Know that I miss you dearly. I wish that I was writing happy news. I know that even if you do not want to see us anymore, you have your reasons. But I feel my obligation to tell you what is happening in our family.

I will get straight to point. I don't know what happen between you and Ezra, but he did tell me that you rejected his proposing. Knowing something of what happened between your father and me, I'm sure you know that I can relate to wanting to be independent and think for yourself and your own future. Whatever the case, Ezra eventually move on and he marry a lovely girl. She is called Caroline. The two of them have a sweet little boy, Justin. When I tell you what happen over the last few weeks, you simply will not believe! Even as I write this, my hand trembles because I can't believe it is true. Justin, just four years old, and the most adorable boy you can imagine, went missing one day, in the middle of night while Ezra and Caroline were sleeping and the boy was also in bed. The police finally find his body two weeks later in the woods close to their house, his lips blue. Can you believe? Who would do such thing? The autopsy report just come back, and I can barely write it out. Report says he was strangled to death. I have not been able to get any sleep in all these days, thinking of who could have possibly wanted to hurt that sweet boy.

Well, just yesterday, a new development in case, which I just will never believe is true. The cops search the house and find among Caroline's clothes in her dresser the tiny little locket that has the pictures of Ezra as a little boy and Caroline as a young girl. Everyone knows that this is locket that is so precious to little Justin. That sweet boy refuses to let anyone take off of him, even when he takes bath! I just cannot for a second believe that she would do that to her own child! Why? I saw them just last year for holidays and she could not have loved that boy more! But you know how the cops are. They took her away and now we are trying to get money together for the bail and waiting for trial where I hope this will all be cleared up.

Please think some good thoughts for Ezra and his Caroline during this whole nightmare. I know you are so busy with your important work, but I hope that I can hear from you, if only to help console my peace of mind. You are our only hope.

Love,
Ma

Even though I had not thought of the thing in so long, I had no doubt in my mind who it was that had caused this disastrous end for such an innocent child. It had been sixteen years since I thought of that fateful night when I left that infant deserted and hideous on the ground outside the hospital where Hana died. It had been sixteen years since I thought about what Ezra had done with his foolish vengeance, and how I had enabled Ezra's darkness to live on through me and my ridiculous pride. I had only hoped that the child had not lived long in this life, having left it in the woods with just a sheet for warmth. It was a shameful wish, but one I believed was for the good of mankind.

After a wretched sleep, I woke to a beautiful spring day, but it was not one that I could enjoy. I was now marked with the blood of two people on my hands, and no one to share this evil with, for who would believe me? I could just imagine how my mother would look at me if I explained what Ezra had done and told her how I had abandoned this monstrous child in the woods. If she did believe me, a scenario I could not envision as remotely possible, would she have me sequestered in a psychiatric ward? Maybe it's what I deserved. But what good would that have done? Ezra would still be out there. The demon I had created would still roam the streets seeking revenge for its wretched life. I rationalized that it would not stop until I was able to find out what it wanted.

Feverish and somewhat delirious from the contents of my mother's letter, I called into work to tell my staff I could not support them that day as I had a family emergency requiring my immediate attention. I almost laughed out loud over the phone, thinking how banal a phrase that suddenly appeared, and yet no other seemed more appropriate. I stole into the very same grove I had sought out so many years ago to cradle the dark, dirty secret of my ambition. I couldn't imagine that it would still be there after all this time, but I couldn't think of anywhere else to start my search.

I knelt next to the patch of dark earth that once held my creation. I placed my hand on it gently, with a vulnerability I wished I had been able to grant my own child, if a child you could possibly call it. I tried to imagine what it would look like now, how much more hideous it had become in the last sixteen years, but it only caused me further anguish. As I rose from my position on the ground, I heard a rustling behind me. I darted around quickly, certain it was the blood I had rejected so long ago. I could barely make it out, but what I saw frightened me. It was an enormous shadow concealed by a copse of trees. The mysterious form was the size of a wild bear but had the height of a giraffe. I was absolutely convinced it was my creation, dark and twisted as I would never have anticipated. I was barely able to take in all of its dimensions before the shadow suddenly vanished, and I was left alone in the woods again.

Z

When it finally came time for Caroline's trial, I must have appeared as though it were me whose life was at the mercy of a panel of jurors and a crowd of onlookers peering through the squares of glass to catch the latest case to satisfy their itch. I hadn't slept a wink since I'd read my mother's letter and learned of the first victim lost at the hands of my creature. Perhaps I should have just come out with it and confessed it was my own hands that led to the loss of an innocent child. How was it that the hideous demon got to roam free while this young boy was now buried in the very ground this thing scours for food and targets? When I arrived in court that morning to see what fate awaited Ezra's wife and the mother of his dead child, I must have appeared to be the very look of a living nightmare. And yet, I imagine that my haggard exterior paled in comparison to the torture I suffered inwardly. Even worse, I could see no recourse to rectify the hell where I now found myself.

It was bizarre, to say the least, that the first time I should have the occasion to meet my sister-in-law, she would be sitting before a judge and jury that was deciding her destiny as the accused murderer of her vulnerable toddler, remarkably close to the same age Ezra was when I first gazed upon him so many years ago. The world where we met and traded affections and love for one another was absolutely unrecognizable in this new landscape of horror. I couldn't imagine a world in which joy and love were once bestowed upon me. It is quite something to reflect upon that life now, as I know that I, too, can blame no one but myself for choosing ambition over a union with others. But it is useless to mourn that now. That life is long gone.

I could see that not so long ago, Caroline held the countenance of a lovely woman. Her hair was tangled in a matted lump and stuck out several inches past her face. Deep pools of a bluish tint hung underneath her eyes, revealing how poorly she had slept since her arrest. She hung her head ever so slightly. I could see that Ezra was quite affected by how quickly she had unraveled, but I was, as yet, unsure if he was aware of the creation he had helped bring to life, the root of ruin to his family, or if he believed her to be the sudden catalyst for all of this torment he now faced.

For the most part, Caroline remained calm and silent during the trial's proceedings, until the moment the prosecution showed the courtroom the photograph of little Justin's body lying lifeless on the ground. At that point, Caroline began to rave and jerk wildly in her chair, taking on the appearance of a raging animal, until the judge wielded threats that succeeded in controlling her. Ezra couldn't take seeing what had happened to his wife, that much was clear, and as she thrashed against her chair, Ezra brusquely walked out of the courtroom. I sat at the edge of one of the rows. When he breezed past me, air from underneath his jacket washed over me. But he seemed to not even recognize me, even when we were inches apart. When he returned, he sat in the back of the room, speaking to no one, his eyes hollowed out and numb. His wife insisted upon her innocence throughout her testimony on the stand, claiming she had no idea how the boy's locket ended up with her possessions inside the house. I could tell by the expressions on the faces of the jurors that they anticipated a more convincing justification from the defendant, some sort of plausible theory as to why the authorities had found the piece of jewelry with her possessions. Before she left the stand, her attorney gave her the opportunity to express anything that had been left unsaid.

"I know it is hard to believe I am innocent of these charges, given this one detail about the locket that my little darling boy has worn every day of his young life," she began, looking at the jury. Her focus was steadfast, but her trembling jaw gave her away.

"But, all I can tell you is I have no reason to kill my own child, who is my whole life and reason for being. I wish I knew what it was the murderer wanted, or why they want to frame me for such a horrendous act against a creature that came from my own body, who captured my whole heart from the first minute his sweaty cheek rested against my breast. I can only assume the murderer was not of sound mind, but I have no earthly idea who this foul monster is. I can't imagine what it would want with me or my child. I only urge you to have sympathy for me and to consider in your hearts what possible motivation I could have for committing such an act. If you have no answer, then I plead with you to find me not guilty."

I found myself so moved by this plea I began to weep, even when I had so many reasons to wish only ill on Ezra. Ezra, who had not laid so much as one eye on me, flicked his gaze towards me, only for a moment, and then went back to staring at his wife with the same blank expression. I did not only cry for Caroline, who was but a proxy for my own misdeeds, but also for the lost children Ezra and I once were. And I cried for Justin, the little innocent child I had never known, the sibling of that creature who ultimately brought him to his death.

Caroline's testimony was not enough to sway the jury or judge. She was sentenced to life in prison without parole. I hoped that there was some sort of appeals process Caroline could file to alter her sentence, but less than a week after her verdict, my mother, who I spoke to briefly at the trial, called me on the phone to tell me in an eerily numb affect that Caroline had hung herself in the early hours of the morning in her holding cell. Ezra was so distraught my mother took him to the old country house to care for him in his time of grief. I don't know if he ever knew it was his own child that was the true criminal responsible for this act, his own sabotage behind the criminal's life and creation.

It was still hard to believe that my creation, which I had once thought would fill the world with progress and future joys, could be the site of so much wreckage. Where I had yearned to create life, only death followed in its place. There was no one I could go to with this knowledge, for anyone I attempted to explain this to would simply call me a raving lunatic. Most everyone would see me as a hysteric woman gone mad. I also knew that Ezra, even if he did have some insight into who might have done this, would certainly take his secret to his grave, especially now that it had caused the losses of both his child and his spouse. This is how my tale of destruction, spun forward from my own bloody hands, began, with these two victims of my own creation, and thus, my own victims as well.

Z

What could I say about what happened? My mind reeled. I felt that the universe had supplied me with gifts of intellect and privilege only to throw them in my face with stark vengeance. Since I was a young child, I had been surrounded by so many men of great regard and brilliance. Why was it that they should live such noble, carefree, empowering lives, and my one hope to make a name for myself and to provide others with the gift of life should come crashing down like Hokusai's *Great Wave*?

I began to spiral, fixating on all the possible scenarios that could have led down a different path to the excitement of new life rather than what lay at my feet instead. If only I had started more simply or paid for more thorough security. If only I had kept Ezra out of my business and my life. If only my father, a monster of his own accord, had not decided to destroy my life beyond the grave. If only, if only, if only. For a brief moment, I contemplated whether or not it was a mistake to refuse Ezra's proposal. Perhaps if I had married him, he would have been satiated enough not to destroy my life's work. But when my thoughts began to travel down that pathway, I was reminded of his ultimate goal: To steal my life's work, to turn me into his servant. As always, the thoughts carried me back to my lost love, my Hana. She was all I wanted. And I had allowed her to get taken down by my hideous ambition, too.

Thoughts of Hana led me to seek out her spirit in comfort, even if I couldn't reach her in person. I drove a few miles out of the city to the creek by the woods where I had scattered her ashes a few days after her memorial. By the time Hana died, no one besides her parents knew that we had ever reunited, as we hoped to surprise my family with our romantic union once we had ushered the perfect child we imagined would accompany us into the world. Hana's family only knew what had happened after Ezra's heinous act.

At the memorial, I told everyone Hana died of complications from childbirth. I did not invite my family to attend. I told Hana's family, who I suspected knew everything up until the delivery, that the child had died at birth. It was hard to tell whether they believed me or not. I wept uncontrollably at the service. Silber attended. I found her expression of grief striking but didn't give the moment much attention, as I was far too centered in my own grief and guilt to notice much of anything else.

At the creek, so long after her death, I ran my hand through the freezing, rushing water with my eyes closed, trying to imagine I was touching Hana herself with my fingertips, even though she was not available to me in human form. Making sure no one could hear me, I implored her to help me, sobbing hysterically as I told her about the monster that killed her, that it had taken two bodies from the earth in addition to her own. I expelled all the demons I'd held in my body for so long. As I screamed each torment into the breeze, caught by the creek that took it under, into its current, I could feel all the pains fall from my body—my stomach unclenched itself, the tension in my face released, and my breath grew in dimensions, losing its shallow, raspy quality. But the healing powers of unloading my pains onto the Hana I couldn't see only made me feel that much worse about all the deaths on my back. How did I deserve to exorcise these lost souls after what I had done to uproot them from the earth? Although my torment was briefly alleviated, the minute I emptied it into the water, the water, like a tide, threw them right back. It seemed there was no end to my dismay, because there was no decision I could make that would undo this monster's destruction or prevent it from hastening.

That is, until the following morning.

At first, I thought it was a dream, just one of my many recurring nightmares about the fiend since it had first been pulled, enormous and bloody, out of my love's protruding belly. I heard the quaking of thunderous steps outside my house while I slept fitfully, a sleep to which I had grown accustomed. Given what a paranoid disaster I had become in the wake of Caroline and Justin's deaths, I didn't pay it much mind at first. I assumed I was merely hearing things, or perhaps it was just the house making its usual shifts and creaking noises as it settled. I went, fitfully, back to sleep.

But then, as I began my day early the next morning, I could swear I witnessed a gargantuan shadow flit past my kitchen window. My pulse raced, my heart quickened its beat in my chest. Finally, it was unmistakable. Three resounding thumps on my front door so deep and loud that a saucer danced on the kitchen counter before it fell to the floor with a shatter. My initial impulse was to ignore the visitor purely out of fright. It couldn't be, I thought to myself. How could it be? Why would the horrific thing make it so easy for me to find? As I tried to determine what I should do, three more thunderous raps beat on the door.

I darted up and looked through the peephole. I couldn't even see a face. All I could see was a piece of fabric, torn and damaged. I reasoned that there wasn't much I could do at this point if it were indeed the demon standing at my door. If it were coming to kill me, perhaps I would finally feel relief to leave this torturous life. I certainly wouldn't be able to outrun it. The only thing left to do was answer.

If someone told me the story of what had stood before me I would not believe them. It was indeed the miserable wretch I had created. It stood barefoot wearing a tattered, wrinkled tunic that seemed fashioned from endless yards of muslin, shorts made from the same material. Its eyes were the piercing blue I had manipulated science for, but in this fashion they felt like the eyes of some supernatural being. It was an enormous creation, maybe eight feet tall, if not taller, its stature made more horrific by its size. Covering its dark blonde complexion I still remembered from its infancy was a thick layer of red hair on its arms, legs, and chest, even its cheeks and forehead, which were spotted with small bubbles of fresh acne and scars I recognized from picking my own blemishes as a teenager. Its hands were four times the size of an ordinary person's, and its feet, which had been of a more normal size when it was born, had grown to match its hands. Its legs almost reached up to its breasts, which were massive and hung loosely in its makeshift shirt, but it was unclear whether the breasts were enlarged pectoral muscles or breasts. Because I had never seen this creature as human, it had never mattered to me whether it had female or male reproductive organs. Perhaps it had both.

The being said nothing as I spent several minutes taking in its appearance and gargantuan size; I assume it was used to such stares and bold objectification. After some time, the shock began to settle somewhat, and I came back to some version of myself, remembering who this demon was. This was the demon who cost my darling Hana her life, who killed a small boy and inadvertently caused his mother's suicide! But if it was coming to kill me, it was what I deserved. I was no longer afraid of my own death after so many other deaths had already happened due to my negligence and self-interest.

"So. It's you. I knew it. How on earth did you manage to cobble out a life after I left you in the woods to die?! You are wretched and you killed a small innocent child for nothing! Kill me if you must, but I have not a word to say to you." I spat at the creation I had hoped so long ago to envelope with love rather than contempt. The creation that I had imagined for so many years would be the center of my greatness, that would help me climb heights that no woman had ever seen. But all that was gone now. This was all that remained of my ambitions. The creation didn't flinch at what I said, but merely gazed upon me for several long minutes of silence. Its next words surprised me.

"I do not want to kill you. I am not ready to hear you say anything. But, look. I once had love in my heart, love that could have been fostered if you had shown me any kindness or humanity. I beg you, if you will do nothing else for me, if you will not love me or cherish my existence that you yourself caused, please, at the very least, listen to my tale. I have but one small request. I will not force you to grant it, but I sincerely ask that you at least hear it through before you deny me. It is the least I deserve."

It took my lack of response as agreement and gestured for me to follow it outside of my small house. We ran through the woods until we came to its hiding place, a structure built of twigs and branches that offered some protection from the weather. It was here that it began to tell me its tale.

Ash

Like the story after which you named yourself and who I can thank for my dreadful existence, this story I am about to tell you, of who I am and how I came to be, I assembled from fragments of memories and half-told anecdotes. The way I came to this world was so haphazard and fractured I can't ever be sure what is the true story of how I ended up here, in this alienated form. But it's the best I have, and so I'll take it on its face or feel no ground beneath my feet for the rest of my days. Sometimes who you are is something you have to decide on, whether it's true or not.

Despite this business of how terrible men have been to you and the world, I find it ironic that it would be a man to save me, mother me, and provide the nourishment and love you denied me. His name was Pine. Now, certainly, that wasn't the name given to him at birth, but it was the name he chose for himself, honoring the shelter that mothered him when his family couldn't give him what he needed. I never knew the whole story, but it wasn't my place to inquire. Besides, I could tell any value his origin story once held was long gone. I can only hope to embody the same, one day.

All I ever knew was that this man who took care of me was called Pine, and he lived in the forests not far from where I would later learn I was born. Pine didn't really know how to be among people anymore, so he flitted from forest to forest, staying in a single place as long as he felt safe from harm and exposure. When I was young, he told me great tales of the many adventures he experienced, the many trees that offered him refuge—from as far west as California and Washington, as far north as Vermont and even Canada. He hadn't lived in the forests where you abandoned me as a newborn long, maybe half a year at most, having traveled south months earlier to find a warmer climate that would shield him from the harsher winters up north. But he'd been living in the woods for many years, and he knew how to make do, how to scavenge for food and clothes and other necessities. Since I had been left in the wild at only a few days old, I would never know the difference between living in the outdoors and the cozy comforts of a house. I'm sure if Pine hadn't found me, I'd be as far underneath the earth as that baby boy I strangled in my rage.

As I grew older, Pine would tell me the story of how we came to be together, how he became both my mother and my father, the only protector I would ever know. Late one night he emerged from his hiding place deep in the woods as he did every night—to search the nearby dumpsters for leftover food or gather loose change that had fallen from someone's pockets onto the asphalt of the parking lot. As he neared the lot, he heard a baby cry in the black dark. At first, Pine worried he would be found and that the cry had signaled others nearby. He was concerned someone would see him and call the police to arrest him. After all, he'd been through this before, many times. But his curiosity got the best of him. He crawled on all fours, like the animals he shared the woods with, following the infrequent sound of human life. To his surprise, Pine came upon a little bundle wrapped tight in a white sheet nestled against the knot at the base of the tree trunk that shared his own name. The man from the woods looked to his left and right, and then out into the dark before him, squinting his eyes to catch the blurry shape of shadows nearby. But Pine saw no one—not an adult running from the scene of this young child's abandonment nor one coming towards the child in relief and wanting. The baby was on its own.

Pine's hunger would have to wait. Taking in this small child, he felt something like kinship with this little babe left in the forest, having no one or thing but the woods to comfort them. Convinced they were completely alone and that he was safe from being found out, he came upon the little crying creature, and gingerly lifted them from the hard, flat ground. At first, the baby cried even more, so hard that their voice hiccupped in their wailing. Their face turned a bright red from the effort they took to expel the fear and longing they felt to be in contact with their parent that was not to be found.

When Pine brought the baby to his chest, he was taken aback at first by how weighted the child already felt in his arms, how large their head, how unusual their appearance. But Pine knew a thing or two of what it meant to be shunned from the world. If Pine allowed others to witness him, what would they think of his ratty hair adorned with twigs and the carcasses of dead insects, the shifting wild gaze caught in his hazel eyes? Perhaps this defenseless young creature is just what Pine had always needed: A companion in the woods that could help be a lookout as they got older or who Pine could teach the ways of the forest to, and thus, they could understand and love one another. Pine thought the longing to be in communion with another had passed so long ago, and yet, excitement grew in him at the idea of having a child to love and belong to, to teach and cradle, as he had always hoped to have been loved and comforted, once.

And so it was that I was saved. Pine became my guardian and protector, and for many years, we were inseparable. He taught me how to read and write and speak from a very early age, and he always made sure to tell me the truth about any question I asked. When he was able to forage in supermarket dumpsters for thrown out jars of baby food, it was a treat that helped me through the rocky terrain of growing up among the elements and without substantial shelter. Otherwise, it was Pine who, like the mother of an animal, chewed up berries and nuts mixed with his spit to feed me so I wouldn't choke in my early years. This enabled me to get the nutrition I needed when I was still a baby. Somehow he was able to get milk for me often enough in those early days, but given the rate at which I inevitably grew, I wonder if it would have been better for us both if he had not been so resourceful after so many years of practice in this life. As I got older I learned, through Pine's example and his teachings, how to be scrappy and adaptable. Later, I would find I would need to fend for myself with or without his help, as I would not be able to rely on him for as long as I had initially hoped.

Ash

Because Pine and I banded together against the world, I did not come of age in the gender binary world that you and all other welcome bodies are accustomed to. As Pine taught me to read and write, he also gave me what neither you nor my father, if father he could be called, could give—a name that befits my particular way of being. The name he gave me came from his understanding and love of all that I was, but the occasion that caused me to finally possess my own name was born of such torment as you will never experience.

On this particular afternoon, Pine had gone to scavenge for supplies and soup when I began feeling feverish from a cold after a few days of hard rain. The rain had let up at this point, and so, bored and curious as young children often are, I began to explore the woods a bit more than I did when Pine watched over me. I took a stick with me and a handful of small pebbles so that I could trace a line in the dirt and drop the pebbles where I wandered to easily find my way back to our shoddy and makeshift camp. I discovered a small stream I had never seen before, as I had never traveled this far, that cut through the woods.

I leaned over the cold stream to run my hands through the water, excited at a new sensation. I was, perhaps, seven years old at this point, and although I had some innate sense I was growing larger more quickly than expected—Pine had to frequently replace my torn and tattered clothes and figure out different strategies to keep my feet protected—this was the first time I remember being faced with my own reflection. It is no understatement to say the face that stared back at me in the folds of blue absolutely terrorized and frightened me.

At first, I couldn't make sense of what I was seeing. The monstrous figure, shadowy but clear enough to discern its hideousness, couldn't possibly be my own reflection! I whipped my head around, hoping I would see another figure behind me, one to account for this confrontation, but I was alone. I didn't interact enough with others to understand what beauty was exactly, but I had read enough in all of the books Pine gave me that I was not filled with any sense of peace or comfort at glimpsing my own lopsided face, the grotesque proportions of my body, or the strange copper hair that covered every inch of my skin.

I fixated on the image that stared back at me for so long that I lost track of time, my hysterical tears falling down my threadbare clothes and dropping into the water below, the thing responsible for the sight of ugliness. Finally, Pine found me—I suppose he followed the line I cut into the dirt. It did not take him long to figure out what had happened, as he noticed my expression that held the depths of pain I felt at viewing how wretched I imagined I looked to all others. He held me for a long time, saying nothing at all, and for this I will always be grateful, for he knew there were no words of denial he could offer to appease me. My worst thoughts were irrefutable.

After I had cried all the tears left in me, at least on that day, he sat me down and spoke with me about what he had been able to find out about where I came from.

"I have waited many years to tell you who it is you come from because I wanted to be sure, and because I wanted you to be old enough to understand the complexities of your birth. Your story is not like the others," Pine said, holding my hand as we sat on the hard, plain ground beneath us. Although I felt soothed by his touch as always, I knew it came with something dark and terrible that I would need to be comforted for, and so, in this moment, his touch frightened me.

"I had a sense that when I found you, you were only a few days old. There is a hospital not far from here, and I figured one of your parents had left you here shortly after your birth." He paused.

"There is a kind man that works at the hospital, who has often given me used uniforms and shoes, leftover food from the food court that would have gone to waste. I have known him a long time and have always been grateful to him. He is someone I know that I can trust. So I asked him if he would try to find out if there was a child that was delivered shortly before the day that I found you, and if he could find out any information for me." Pine briefly took his hand back and wiped his face. He grabbed his old worn backpack behind him, and pulled out some pieces of paper with text printed on them.

"Before I give this to you, I want to tell you the story. I want it to come from someone who loves you. These people responsible for your birth do not matter anymore. I love you, and you are safe. And that is all that matters. Your parents are both scientists, and although they are not blood-related, they lived together in the same family for many years. The woman who carried you does not share your DNA, but she would have been a loving parent to you, if she could have found it within herself to care for you. I think, based on this letter, she would have. She died during complications of childbirth." He paused. "Many people in the world get hung up on ambition. They lose sight of what's important." He stroked my long, greasy hair and cupped his hand around the back of my neck. "You have always been such a treasure to me. If you know anything, know that."

He held a letter from Silber, who, as you know, was the midwife at my birth, addressed to Pine's friend, whose name was David Black. He and Silber were not close, but because Silber's clients often ended up, for one reason or another, needing to be admitted to the hospital for safer births than she could provide, they had grown fond of one another. David had a feeling that Silber might know something of what had happened to this mysterious child Pine spoke of, and so he reached out to her. She was grateful to be asked after so many years about the most tragic case she had worked in all of her years as a midwife. In fact, losing Hana in such a disastrous way had struck her so deeply that she never returned to midwifery and changed occupations altogether. Silber wouldn't discover until a few days after Hana's death that Hana had sent her a letter shortly before she went into labor, telling her all that had transpired to bring me into the world. Hana had predicted that she might not make it through the delivery. She assumed rightly that you would never tell anyone what had happened, and so she left this knowledge with Silber, a woman she trusted, and the only one she imagined would keep this story safe, until it was the right time to reveal it.

This letter told the entire story of how I was conceived and delivered. I learned I live with a condition called gigantism, due to a genetic mutation that came from both you and my father. It was this day I learned who you were, and through Hana's letter, I also found out what Ezra had done to cause you to scorn my birth. I discovered Ezra did not just want revenge for being rejected. It was his greed, like my grandfather's, that caused him to lay claim to everything he sought and that was also the agent which destroyed my chance at beauty and happiness in the real world. Both of you were responsible for the source of my repugnance, the reason I had been abandoned and left to die.

I felt great sadness for my mother, Hana, carrying me against her will only to lose her life at the end, and tremendous guilt that it was my body that killed her. At the same time, I was unspeakably grateful to Silber for her generosity and willingness to share my story with another and for David to share her story with Pine, who shared it with me. Without a story of where you come from, how do you understand the ground beneath you that holds your feet?

In Silber's letter, she wrote that Hana spoke of your calalai, a word I had never heard before but was intrigued by. I didn't know I was part Malay and Chinese, that my grandmother grew up in Indonesia. It gave me great happiness to learn my birth story. Pine used this conversation as an opportunity to talk about what it meant to be male and female, and how Pine had learned long ago to reject the constraints of societal dictates of gender and race and everything else in between. Pine offered me a name to hold onto, like a home where none could be found. Not for someone like me. Not for someone like Pine. He asked how I felt about the name Ash. Pine explained how the word signified both the body of a tree and also the absence of it, and that he'd read that ash trees are at once male and female, flower and tree.

It was perfect. Not only did it resonate with my split and liminal nature, but I loved its connection to the only person who had ever loved me. It would always remind me of Pine, the only family I'd ever hoped to find. From that point on, I had a name to call my own, a name to remind me of where I came to live, in the middle of the woods, and where I first found love. I wanted to live with Pine forever, but I would discover that my mutant body and self would keep me from that constant, too.

Together we found a suitable singular pronoun that wasn't gendered, one that came from my grandmother's birth-land of Indonesia: Dia. I liked the sound of it. I thought, if I ever were to be in a situation in which a pronoun would need to be used for me, if I ever became part of the world, this would be the pronoun I would use. It felt perfect given my dual-gendered self, my thinginess. I told Pine this immediately. He smiled and assured me if there was ever a need for him to refer to me in the third person, he would make sure to address me in the way I desired.

As I was reading about your calalai, I came across the word *bissu*, which technically translates to transvestite priest but has evolved over the modern age in South Sulawesi to describe someone intersex or even metagender. When Pine and I read about bissu, we both looked at one another at the same moment, and we knew. This was me. I rolled the word around on my tongue, smiling, feeling squishy and soft in my body as I uttered it. And so, I tell you now that my name is Ash, and I am a bissu, and I hope you can understand why, in all future cases both within my company and beyond it, I want to be referred to by the pronoun dia.

Let me tell you what happened after Ko left me. I wasn't like her. I didn't share the life or parents she had. I knew there was no way I could come back after I left—*so disrespectful*, 討厭,[29] I imagined Ba saying under his breath, or perhaps even shouting out into the void of all the rooms of the house he once called for me to fill with my badness.

Once Ko left, I was frozen in despair, frightened to make my next move without her.

I didn't have time to grieve. I had to figure out what it would take for me to survive the world without an other to huddle with under a tarp in the rain, or a ba to shelter and clothe me, whether it came accompanied by the sting of a hand or without it. But I'd taken myself on this path, and I had to follow it through to the other side.

And so, like Frank's creation, I wandered the forests,

---

29 tǎoyàn

too. I became friends with the trees and the dirt and the sky. I learned how to maneuver around the sudden torrential rains of the South, the sun's blazing breath. The trees were fine company, offering me shelter and sustenance. They never forsook me or abandoned me when I needed them most, like Ko, or even Ma. They never struck me down when I misbehaved like Ba did.

For a time, I felt at home; at least, the only home I had come to know as one that offered me all I could need and never disappointed.

I wasn't always alone either. There was Maisie, a runaway from who knows where—we tree dwellers had an unwritten code never to ask one another where we came from or how we came to be in the streets and the woods—with thick blonde matted hair and a pup named Scout. We instantly bonded just half a year after Ko left, but we knew our connection wasn't permanent. It couldn't be, as living in the forest was too risky in big numbers.

There was Hunter, who felt it important to tell his story—to whoever he came across under makeshift tents in the woods—of loss. We could all relate to the journey of losing. Hunter had been taught to be the enemy, trained to hack down trees and kill the families of deer and rabbits that feared the target of his family's bullets, the engine of their truck whirring in the street next to where they slept, on the prowl. He grew to hate the thirsting blood that was his legacy, and when it became clear that as long as Hunter lived under his father's roof, he'd have no choice but to axe down the elegant pines and oaks on his family's property and turn the animals that lived there into carcasses stripped of their meat for Sunday night dinner, he knew there was no way out but to run. He changed his name to Hunter so that it was never a dark secret where he came from, but a scar on his body he hoped would forever remain in his past. Hunter's skills, which he offered gladly, knowing what his family owed the world that was now his refuge, came in handy. When he turned his hands over, palms upward, one arm showed a tiny tattoo of a hunting rifle and the other a tender stick-and-poke illustration of Copper, his favorite wild fox his father hunted down and killed for sport just because he could, because he knew what meaning Copper held for his son.

I met many more misfits like Hunter and Maisie who, for one reason or another, could no longer make it work in the civilized world. We were all connected by the vast universe of trees we found ourselves under, tied together by the loss we tried to carve out of our bodies and fill with something else, something safe. For it was true that we felt safer in the woods—dirty and hungry and tired and hiding from the train track of a cop's flashlight trying to aim its beam at us as if it were as destructive as the rifle of Hunter's father, as if we were meat waiting to be emptied for its use—than we did in our own homes.

I learned it didn't matter if I was different there. It didn't matter how filthy or threadbare my clothes were, how cut open my toes that fit through the holes in my shoes. No one cared I wasn't like them, in skin or whose touch I craved. All of us gave to one another openly and evenly, without question or disgust. I never had to worry about being 討厭[30] here. No black, angry eyes seethed at me like Ba's for tracking dirt on the brand new carpet or for getting a lower score on a report card than he demanded.

I could just be, and here, being was enough.

I only wished it could have lasted. I wish that, for me, it could have been enough for always. But I had dreams that went far beyond what the forest or my misfit family could give me. I would always be Ba's daughter, with hopes and ambitions of making something of myself that could be embraced by the world I wished I no longer needed. I was both monster and scientist, and I wanted to be lover and maker.

---

30 tǎoyàn—loathed with disgust

Ash

Pine and I spent a few more years together before the peculiar circumstances of my monstrosity and development would force my only companion and guardian, the only love I ever knew, to leave me as well. Before that point, however, Pine would give me the gift I would soon realize I needed most in this world as a shield for survival, that of knowledge and insight.

Each week, Pine would sneak into the city library closest to whatever forest was our home at that particular time and bring back books he felt would help me with my idiosyncratic nature. I didn't know it at the time, but now I realize he was also giving me the tools to live apart from him, to manage on my own in this dark and cruel world. Pine taught me how to read and write when I was very young, so that by the time I was an adolescent, I was reading classic and contemporary texts far advanced for my age. Sometimes we read the texts together, but as I became more intellectually curious and reading became an elixir I could drink on my own and lose myself in, he would leave me to the books themselves while he searched for food for us or took care of other necessary chores. When I reached a stopping point, we would come back together and he would discuss the text's important concepts with me, asking me guiding questions for as long as I needed them. By the end of our scholarly journey, I would synthesize the ideas and integrate them into how I viewed myself and the world. He merely watched me, listening with enraptured attention and casting an affectionate gaze upon me.

He taught me Du Bois's notion of double consciousness, making sure I understood the Black American context from which it was fashioned but also how it could provide insight into my many layers of identity. We read *Black Boy* and *Invisible Man*, the works of Frederick Douglass and Huey Newton. It was hard to swallow the long, agonizing journey of Black men in America, especially when they came with only a skin color that was not associated with whiteness and did not even have the hideousness of my body that continued to become more grotesque by the minute. He stopped me in that self-delusion and tried to educate me on the dangers of equating the feelings I had of my physical nature with that of what Black men, women, trans, and nonbinary lives dealt with from moment to moment in this country and many, many others. I was too young to fully take it to heart, but I would later understand this more, as I was fortunate enough to live on the edges of society in ways so many others couldn't.

We read Angela Davis and bell hooks, Audre Lorde and

Octavia E. Butler, and of course, James Baldwin. I labored through Nell Irvin Painter's *The History of White People* and was inexplicably drawn to Claudia Rankine. I was taken with Baldwin's queerness and Lorde's explication of biomythography and wondered if one day, I, too, could write my own myth of my own body, selfhood, and history into being like she did. We read so many other texts about racism and the history of segregation, and when the histories and ideologies framing those books became too heavy for my mind, we switched to Susan Stryker and Adrienne Rich, Judith Butler and Jack Halberstam, Janet Mock and José Esteban Muñoz, and general texts like *Genderqueer* and *Queer: A Graphic History*. These voices taught me more about my body, which I hoped would be accepted by society one day.

After I read all that Pine found on what it meant to live between he and she, girl and boy, I asked for language guidebooks on Indonesian and Malay, knowing their relationship to my heritage and legacy.

Books were a world where I could leave behind the demonic nature of my body, even as it grew exponentially with every word that I read. We wouldn't only read serious books, though. Pine also introduced me to the most exquisite storytellers and poets that I would turn to again and again for solace and for a way out of the confining life I never asked to be given.

What a wretch I was that the only way I could feel happy was to consume words that would make me feel I had left the world completely! I felt tremendous guilt and ambivalence about this, but I took what pleasure I could from the pursuits I found that would help me forget how, with each passing day, I would become larger and larger, taller and taller, and more and more separate from Pine. It was tormenting to feel so far away from him. I wanted to mirror him as a young child mirrors dia parent, but I could see that with each inch that I swelled in any direction, Pine grew increasingly anxious and agitated from its results. It was becoming ever more difficult to clothe me, and our privacy and protection were harder to hold on to, as I became more and more visible, my body exploding far beyond the broad expanse of even the largest trees that cloaked us from the authorities.

It hadn't quite struck me yet, however, that there would ever be a world in which Pine and I weren't eternally connected to one another as we always had been. I could feel the stress my horrid countenance caused him, but it never occurred to me Pine would ever feel he would have to leave me. He gave me so much nurturing and support, so much love and understanding, I believed fully in his ability to conquer any obstacle. I felt tremendous guilt and shame at the difficulties I caused, but they happened of their own accord, and there was nothing I could really do to stop my tremendous growth or even slow down its acceleration.

One day Pine brought me a book on André the Giant, the only person I had ever seen that had an existence and body even remotely like mine. It was a tremendous gift to me, as André, as a man and a profitable athlete, was able to have the support that I couldn't imagine would ever grace my bizarre physiognomy. Besides, I was made in such an illegal and complex manner that I would never be able to convince anyone to hear my story long enough to help me. I assumed, like the Creature in *Frankenstein*, that anyone who saw me would just attack me with hatred in their hearts. Who would believe me over my maker, anyway? You were vetted and successful and did not look anything like me. If you couldn't even keep me as an infant, how could anyone else take me as I am now?

Ash

Tensions started to build between us, although we never spoke of them. I saw the look on Pine's face when my clothes ripped yet again, or when I grew so quickly out of the shoes he had just finished repairing from the last time. When he was incredibly frustrated, he would groan and mumble under his breath. I held my head downwards. We loved each other too much to quarrel, and after all he had done for me, the least I could do was allow him these moments of agitation. Due to the unwieldy and swelling nature of my grotesque form, we were becoming increasingly vulnerable to the threat of police and other authorities. We had to flee our makeshift homes again and again, being forced to abandon the few items we found in dumpsters and on the curbs of suburban streets, when a group of police officers would come with their lights and their guns.

The condition of my body wasn't my fault, but it's not as though it didn't come without its own dangers. I didn't blame

Pine for his building frustrations or his thinly disguised anger at the spreading pattern of my physical form. It was yet another unhappy circumstance of my inherited condition.

I can still see the agitation that fell across his face from time to time. He tried to hide it from me, but his frustration was becoming more apparent by the day as his admonishment slipped out when I came to him with another split in my pants or a toe peeking out from the shoes he made for me by hand with materials found on the grounds near us. Due to his foraging and constant mending, especially given the varying temperatures outside, the skin on his hands began to peel and crack so deeply even our small tub of stolen Vaseline couldn't fix it.

When I reached adolescence, the growth spurts took on a life of their own. I remember a particular day when I grew out of the oversized shorts Pine had built out of scraps he had found in a dumpster behind a small fabric store, an article of clothing which gave him great pride.

"P?" I tapped him lightly on the shoulder, afraid to tell him I had ripped the seat of the shorts.

"Yes, love?" he asked without much thought, lying on his side on a blanket, reading.

"I need new shorts." I didn't know what else to say. Pine threw his book down and ran to the back of me to investigate. I could feel him pull apart the two pieces of fabric where they were once joined.

"Ash! You need to be more careful. I can't keep doing this for you. One day you are going to have to learn to do this for yourself," he shouted. I ran from him, angry and scared, as far as I could.

"Ash, wait! I'm sorry!" he called out, but his voice fell into a murmur in the distance. My feet beat on the ground with each step, a vibration that ricocheted for miles. The sound only deepened the pain I felt in my heart at this massive form I had been given, at the inconvenience and burden it caused Pine, and you, and everyone.

It was not only his rage that frightened me, but I could feel within myself a kind of devilish response I knew better than to let out of its cage. I was in my adolescence then, and I could already feel the unbridled strength that thrummed within me. If anything were to happen to Pine because of the uncontrollable power within my own body, I would never forgive myself.

I did not return for many hours. I screamed and wept and pounded my large fists into the ground. The day was beautiful and contained, the forests expanded far out from where I sat, taking up so much space in the earth. I could feel it coming. I would never be a form anyone would want.

When I returned that day, Pine and I didn't speak of what happened. He held me for a long time, longer than ever before. We didn't need words. Besides, there was nothing he could say. Nothing that I could do.

There is not much to say about the day Pine finally met his limit and felt he had no other option than to leave me on my own. He didn't warn me or prepare me ahead of time, but I imagine he didn't know how. One morning, I woke up and found I was alone. A folded letter pinned to my pocket.

I wondered how stealthy he had to be so as not to wake me, but, after all, Pine had years of practice in making himself as small and soundless as possible. I don't want to divulge all of the contents of his goodbye—some of what he wrote was just for me, for us—but I'll say it was clear he felt terribly about abandoning me, knowing all I would inevitably face alone, but he also didn't know what other solution there was for his own survival and livelihood. I didn't blame him. I was grateful for all the years he had given to caring for me.

He left me with one last parting gift, which led me here. He gave me your full name and residence so I might find you and confront you, and perhaps learn my story from its source. Maybe there was more of the story to tell beyond what Silber knew, beyond even Hana. Perhaps, Pine hoped, enough time had passed it was possible for my birthparent to truly accept me. He did warn me against exacting revenge. In his experience, he wrote, nothing good ever came of it. But he was an old man by then, and I was a ball of hormonal explosions with no guardian to even attempt to subdue my innermost desires and impulses.

There is no way to adequately communicate the despair, self-hatred, and rage that accompanied my grief over losing the only family and love I have ever known. But it was not Pine who was the target of my rage and burning agony. It was you. You. Why did I live only to be forsaken by my Creator, the only being truly responsible for me? Why did I not have the ability to extinguish myself so that I could be put out of my misery and that of anyone whose path would cross mine? I simply could not make sense of the purpose for which I was put on this Earth and how I could leave this abominable experience.

Pine had taught me enough that I waited to express these feelings audibly until it was late at night so that my howling would be mistaken for that of a rabid animal far into the woods. That was how I spent many, many nights—crying out to the moon like a wolf, wishing for a different body, a different mother, a different existence than the hell that bore a hole inside of me.

But it was not only my Creator who had forsaken me. It was the one that got in, that slipped through the cracks and poisoned me with his seed. Ezra. If Hana had been allowed to give me the sperm to fertilize your egg, then perhaps I would have had a chance at whatever can be called a "normal" life. If I was going to have to exist in this cruel world, with a body that I imagined everyone feared or hated, then the least I could do was make the person truly responsible for my wretchedness suffer even a fraction of what I had endured. I was entitled to it, I reasoned with myself, given what he put me through for his own selfish recklessness and control. Besides, if the world saw me as the monster anyway, I might as well give them the nightmare they imagined me to be.

Once I resolved myself to this end, the late-night howls of loneliness and grief started to subside within my chest, and I was finally able to sleep at night. I felt a slight pang of guilt knowing that Pine would want better for me than this, but I also knew I would undoubtedly never see him again and never be faced with his reaction. Besides, he didn't know what it was like to live in this body, to be abandoned by both my mother and the only love I had ever received. It was a pain with which no one could empathize. There was no semblance of a fulfilling life I could imagine with a hideousness like mine. At least I would feel my abhorrent existence vindicated, the villain punished for his senseless acts.

Ash

How could I possibly articulate the chaotic and conflicting emotions that swirled through my ghastly and enormous form? I had no mother, for you had rejected me before I had even become the height of my monstrousness. Pine, the only father I had ever known, had been forced to abandon me, and Ezra, if father he could be called, had poisoned me with his own life force, only to destroy any chance I would have at a happy and fulfilling life with the two beings in love who had divined to create me in order to bestow on me the epitome of protection and nurturing. And for what? Because he would not get to carry on the dying wish of a man who had abused him? Because he would not get to own his sibling's wealth she had worked so hard in her life to achieve? In my enraged and bereaved haze, I felt he did not deserve an ounce of sympathy I could offer. The only person I truly felt would have loved me was Hana, the mother who carried me in her belly and who died before she had even a chance to rest her eyes on me. Perhaps in that connected state of motherhood, she would have been able to see past my wretchedness.

But I was not only enraged by my cursed creators and the hell they had leashed upon me by bringing me into the world, only to shun me and leave me unrooted, left to the winds of the harsh earth to determine my fate and my survival. It seemed the very fact of my birth and form, one could argue, necessitated an even more crucial need of them. I cloaked myself in mourning for the form my father was responsible for had caused Pine, the one I loved most in the world and the only being I could imagine to offer me sympathy and kindness, to turn away from me in order to maintain his own livelihood.

He simply did not have the resources to clothe me in the way that would best help me move through life. With each day I grew, it became harder and harder to shield both of us from danger, even death. I did not blame him for leaving me behind, but it did not make his loss any less painful or devastating. I could not imagine a scenario in which any other person would embrace me with openness and understanding as Pine had. Never in my entire life had I felt so destitute.

All of the pain I felt at my new life, empty of any human contact or compassion, only fueled me towards my mission of vindicating my spurned existence and life. I had heard Pine speak enough about his stealthy ways of gathering information, such as when he found you and your whereabouts, which led me here. Using his methods I was also able to establish where Ezra lived and the details of his new life with his wife and child. Learning about Ezra's fulfilling and enriching life only injected me with more purpose to wreak havoc on his family, as it infuriated me to know he could move on so easily after the cruelty he had enacted on both of us only to gain the family he always dreamed of without a moment's thought as to what he had destroyed. I wondered, as I scrolled through photos on the local library's computer of Ezra's golden-haired child, my half-brother, and Ezra's wife with the carefree expression plastered on her face in family photos, if he ever thought of me, the demon child he had tainted with his semen and then erased from his life. I was certain his wife knew nothing of his past misdeeds. What caused such abhorrent behavior from such creatures?

As days passed into nights, I wished that the trees that shielded me from rain or the stars that cradled me in the night sky could act as a reprieve from the horrors that lay within my heart. On the contrary, Nature's gifts of beauty and stillness only served to mock my interior state. How could I enjoy such trivial pleasures when I could not have the most basic needs of life—nourishment, companionship, and love? What could a tree or a twilit sky do for me in their absence? Besides, now that Pine was gone, the world that used to be my refuge only made me feel more achingly alone than ever. I knew I had to make my peace with eternal solitude, for there was no one who could comfort me now. Pine was the rarest of birds, and I knew better than to ever hope for another one to land in my path again.

Given my gigantic and conspicuous demeanor, I knew that the best time for me to approach Ezra's house was at night, when they would least suspect any intruders. As they slept soundly in the next room nearby their child, I knew, also, there was less chance that Ezra would instill any kind of alarm to notify him of my presence. Besides, why would he expect any creature to bring harm to him? It was clear from his own actions that he believed he was invulnerable to any threat, human or otherwise. It was this reckless entitlement I hoped to break apart with the body that he himself was responsible for bringing to life.

By the light of the moon, I crept into the backyard of their modest house in the city, scaled its side, and snuck in through the window. Because the little tot was slumbering so deeply, it took no time at all to put my one enlarged hand around his tiny little throat, pinch in one quick movement, and choke his air supply. I did not feel great remorse while I watched his tiny chest no longer rise and fall with each breath, for he looked not that different from when he had been peacefully sleeping only a moment before. I did, however, feel a twinge of resentment looking at his beautiful, predictable form. I simultaneously held in my own mind what I must have looked like at his age, the image swelling larger than the bed that held his dainty figure. I shuddered with sadness and anger. At the same time, I strangely indulged in another fantasy where we lived as siblings in a house just like this one, but I knew that fantasy had no basis in reality. All I wanted was for someone responsible for my suffering to experience even a fraction of what I had endured.

I knew the only way Ezra would truly feel the enormity

of my crime was if I framed him. I wanted him to feel the weight of my torturous existence, and so killing him would not do, for then he would be granted eternal peace in death. As I stared at the boy's chest, I suddenly noticed the small locket that graced the toddler's torso, which contained photos of his parents, a gift I would never fully understand or whose symbolism I could ever appreciate. With a quick pull of my beastly hand, the chain came free, and I made a point to hide it in his wife's bureau the next day—once I had already stowed the child deep in the woods, after rinsing him of my fingerprints in the creek that ran through the forest, but close enough to the house so the authorities would eventually and effortlessly come upon him. My fingerprints wouldn't have mattered anyway; I wasn't a registered person in any system. As a human being, I wasn't acknowledged at all. Without much struggle, I dug through the wet earth in the woods where I planned to place him, hiding him haphazardly under some dirt, his head covered by a bed of damp leaves. I didn't want it to be too difficult for him to be found, so it would be more feasible that a woman without any experience in committing crimes had attempted to hide him.

Before I exited the window with the child, I hesitated briefly, the adrenaline of revenge and torment coursing through my veins. I knew the man responsible for my fiendish form slept just a few feet from where I stood. I wondered what would simmer within me if I were to come upon his face, one I had envisioned in the heat of my hatred for so many years. But I knew it was not the time to confront him—only when I had stripped him of all his feelings of power, happiness, and comfort did I want him to be able to see me in full view. To realize just what his decision had done to his perfect fantasy.

After I snuck back into the house the following evening, knowing it would be empty while the occupants were searching the woods for their child, I gingerly placed the locket in his wife's dresser, making sure not a hair was left out of place in the rest of the house. I lingered a moment, resting my eyes on the photos framed on the mantle and scattered on various walls, trying to imagine what it must be like to have the life initially intended for me before Ezra committed his one grievous action to make it go so awry.

Once it was clear my revenge would surely enact what I had hoped for, it was time to meet my Creator. I now knew what I wanted to say: What I ascertained was the only resolution to this horrific tale.

Ash

The most remorse I felt for my acts of cruelty—although, given the horror of my existence, I did not find the acts that cruel initially—was when I discovered what had happened to Ezra's wife, whose poor soul I inevitably weighed all of my crime's yoke upon. I had wondered if Ezra would question whether it was I, his grotesque spawn, who was capable of such an act. I wondered if he would ever confess to what he had done so many years ago. Perhaps I gave him too much credit, and his denial and repression of who he had been in his young life cut so deep that he truly had erased all knowledge and existence of me from his mind. I did not dare incite the mob by getting close enough to the courthouse to find out. However, I did find abandoned newspapers each night that reported on the trial's events, as it was such a ghastly story that excited the curiosity of everyone in the town.

I saw that you were there, and I wondered, too, if my Creator had discovered that it surely must have been me. Did you feel any sort of sympathy for the monster you had created with your abandonment and refusal of me as your child? I knew it was foolish to assume those responsible for my life would think such things, especially given how many years had gone by. But children always wonder about the beings who forsake them.

Regardless, when I learned Caroline did not even offer an alibi or insist that the prosecution (or the defense, for that matter) scour the ends of the town to find out what villain was truly to blame for the violent loss of her son, I knew she would reach a tragic end. But I never imagined her end would be by her own hand. At worst, I thought she would get life in prison, but good behavior would perhaps cause her to have a different narrative, one in which she would be freed on parole—especially due to the fact that she had an immaculate record up until this unthinkable crime. After all, she was not my true target. I only wanted Ezra to suffer. I should have thought more about what Pine would have wanted for me. I should have realized that vengeance would never give me the satisfaction I craved. That nothing could, barring acknowledgment and acceptance from those who made me. In my mind, that was an impossibility that I could search my whole life in pursuit of only to end up embittered and even more alone.

I needed to think of a new way to be at peace with this hideous existence, this pitiful thing called a life, if life it could be called. What I truly craved was to live out the rest of my days with another soul whose companionship I could have as my own, another soul who would look upon me with tenderness and love. But how could I find another who would see past my ugly physiognomy and accept me as I am? Certainly I could think of no other creature, aside from Pine who was long gone, that would have the kindness of spirit to understand of what, exactly, I was made. It was too risky to seek out another like Pine, who had been fortunate enough to come upon me when I was but a vulnerable and helpless infant and not the large and unwieldy creature I had become. Even André the Giant had fame on his side, an opening for the world to seek to understand him. That is when I realized you were the key, my only chance at attaining true happiness.

If I were to truly find another who would live out the rest of their days with me, there was only one way. I would need a companion made of the same attributes I possess, who could understand my condition as they, too, would suffer from the same circumstance. No one else will have me, and mankind is too obsessed with beauty and wholeness to see through my countenance for what is behind it. I will not leave your side until you create for me a companion or, better yet, a child, one just as I am, who will not refuse me their companionship and kindness and will accept my tenderness and love. Given all you have done to give me this miserable life, this is the one request I am after. I will not take my leave of you until it is granted.

VOLUME TWO

李

We took a break then, Dr. Frank and I, to sit with Ash's harrowing story up to this point. So many thoughts swirled through my mind that at times I felt as if I were spiraling a magical kind of whirlwind, but at others, I wondered if I would end up circling a drain. By the time the scientist got to this point of the story, I could see how she struggled with what had transpired. Although I was desperate to discover if she completed this request for her creation as dia requested, if something more dire had happened as a result of it, I also knew I needed to allow her the space to be with all her story must have brought up for her in telling it to another, especially someone she barely knew.

It seemed otherworldly, though, to become connected to someone whose story intersected with mine in such incomprehensible and surreal ways. I, too, had been in the woods when I felt no one else could have me. I, too, had lived a life surrounded by the made and the maker, the parent and the child, and it provoked so many other questions within me regarding responsibility and abandonment. It was hard for me not to find myself struck with compassion for the creature my idol had made. I questioned Dr. Frank's choice to neglect her child in such a rash and impulsive manner. I couldn't help but see her through a new flare of light that cast a shadow over her tale. How was she different from my own mother who left me as a small child? In fact, Dr. Frank was far worse, as there was no one else, as far as she was concerned, that would have cared for this child instead. Not to mention, this child was quite literally made with the doctor's own hand, an intentional sculpting from the materials available. No accident could be blamed for this conception. What did Hana die for? What was her life worth to Dr. Frank? Perhaps caring for this creature would have been the only thing to make her loss worth something in the end.

The entire tale causes me to reflect on other losses, other absences. I'm unclear whether I, too, abandoned my own ba. Is it possible for a child to abandon a parent? A friend I met while on the streets told me that, due to the difference in power and responsibility from the one made rather than the one who chose to make a defenseless creature they're indebted to care for, a child can't abandon a parent. Not only that, but it isn't possible for an adult to abandon another adult. That it is through the role of parent (or guardian) only that one could be accused of such neglect. Of course, this led me to ponder other aspects of Dr. Frank's story. Can we hold those surrogate parents we meet along the way in our disenfranchised lives responsible in the same ways we expect of our birthparents? Am I allowed to cast judgment on Pine for leaving Ash in dia great hour of need? Is it morally acceptable for me to hold sympathy for the creature when dia was responsible for the loss of two lives that were innocent of the evil that, nonetheless, dia punished them for?

I blame Ma for leaving us. Her abandonment is a hole carved out of my chest that can never be filled by her or any other ever again. But what is there to say about the loss left by parents who are neither wholly present nor fully absent? What absence is there to be felt by Ba, for example, where marks against my skin were the only sign of what some would consider love? Is the strike of violence from parent and child its own form of abandonment?

I found myself moved by Ash's decision—not only to wreak havoc on those who had created dia, a choice I imagine comes from a most desperate state—but also the demand of dia parent, the belief that a creature could trust in the very creator who had forsaken dia. You might ask how I could be so moved by Dr. Frank's story, knowing what I know of it now. I find myself taken by her grief and despair at the actions of her own hands. It's hard to separate from her in the intimate bubble of my apartment, uninterrupted by any intrusions or distractions, to make sense of her own traumatizing choices. Perhaps it's not really about her at all, but about me, and Ko, and Ma. If I believe Dr. Frank is capable of remorse for her own wrongdoing, could that mean, somewhere, in some other reality, Ma might also understand what she did wrong, and my heart can finally gain closure? And yet, I find it hard to remain in Dr. Frank's presence without judging her choice, now that we've been through the story long enough to hear the creature's tale of what it is to live a life spurned and rejected. It's something I must come to, sooner than later, to make sense of what she symbolizes, not just for the world, but for my own story, my own mother, my own cursed creation.

Z

My creation fell silent.

I had hoped for something so much more when I first embarked on the journey to create the perfect specimen, but now, seeing this being standing before me, all I could see was my dream falling so short of my hopes. Not only that, but now this oddity peered deeply into my eyes and demanded that I perform the same cursed act twice! The same immense failure that had destroyed so many lives and cost me so much grief and torture. The devastating choice that had led to the death of my Hana, my love! I had to admit that I was quite moved by its story, but nonetheless, I couldn't imagine what line of logic had led it to this conclusion, and even more, how it thought it remotely possible I would grant its request, given all the destruction it had caused to so many I had once loved.

"You must make me a person. I don't care whether they are male or female. Gender never mattered much to me. I don't care to find romantic love. I've long made my peace with how much less a life I will live compared to all who surround me. But I want you to make me someone I can live out the end of my days with who will understand me, for they will be in the same predicament as I am. I will be able to offer them something no one else will, an understanding of their place in this life, a love in themselves that will go beyond these outdated norms of beauty and ability. Given all you have refused me, this is the least you could do to make this horrific tale livable."

As the thoughtfulness of the creature's tale slowly subsided, I returned to my senses and started to see the wretch in front of me as I had before—a monster incapable of sound reasoning. My skin pulsated and itched with anxiety. Even the air seemed to rush out of the room from fright.

"How could I grant you such an audacious request?" I asked in shock, the words flying out of my mouth without much consideration of the power in the body facing me, how easily it could vanquish me with a flick of one of its gigantic wrists.

"Look at all your deformities caused! A child, a mother, gone forever. Your own sibling! I had assumed you simply did not know that Ezra's boy was connected to you by blood. But you knew! And you still committed this vicious act. If I brought another being like you into the world, how much more torment would it cause the innocent? Perhaps you would only teach it to further harm others as you have already done! *You may render me the most miserable of mankind, but you will never make me base in my own eyes.*[31] You can kill me if you'd like; I can't stop you. But I will never agree to this request. The risk is too great. You are not to be trusted."

A look of calm swept over the monster's eyes, which surprised me, as I expected to finally meet the end of my many years of torture since first looking into this creature's eyes as an infant so many years ago. It smiled with the grin of a madman. I was overcome with nausea.

"I understand how I must look to you, to everyone. But you are still my parent who left me abandoned on a tree stump as an infant, even after all the work you did to create this new life. I don't blame you for who I am now. It isn't, after all, your doing that caused me to become this hideousness I see you cower from in fright. But how do you expect me to live out my days when there is no one to comfort me, sympathize with me, or show me even the smallest kindness? Show me one human being who will keep company with me, and I, too, will remain generous of spirit. But you know you cannot because there is no one in this world, except for Pine, who can provide me with even the smallest connection to sustain myself. Even he could not keep his word to me because of this body of mine. If you do not grant me this request, I will not stop until I have destroyed everyone that you cherish, I can promise you that. That includes your precious lab and all its secrets. Would you blame me?"

As the creature became increasingly heated and agitated,

---

31 Shelley, *Frankenstein.*

its forehead and cheeks creased in lines that distorted its already grotesque face. It terrified me, not merely for its ugliness, but for the rage that quivered within it.

"*It is true, we shall be monsters cut off from all the world; but on that account we shall be more attached to one another. Our lives will not be happy, but they will be harmless and free from the misery I now feel.*[32] Do you remember those lines? They're from *Frankenstein*, your namesake, the source of your inspiration, which you have only used to perpetuate the mythology of the story you sought to dismantle and build anew, albeit without such dreaded consequences."

Its words stung because I could hear the truth in them I did not want to uncover or confront. It was hard to deny the power behind the creature's persuasive plea, that this was my only way out of this whole disaster. If I granted my creation this one last request, would I be free of this sordid tale for the rest of my days? The air in my chest expanded just imagining it. Could I dream of a life beyond this horrid tragedy?

"I promise you that if you provide me a companion, you will never hear or see evidence of either of us ever again. I have no need for any more blood on my hands; my revenge is done, and it cost more than I gained from it. All I have ever wanted was for someone to witness me and embrace me in my despair and torment. To love me despite my form and condition. Like Pine did. Please do not forsake me after you have taken so much from me already. I did not ask to be created; but

---

32 Shelley, *Frankenstein*.

now that I am here, I ask for the basic needs of affection that each being has a right to in this life."

I couldn't believe I was considering this outlandish request, but I was also taken by my own failure and this monster's understandable need for human contact from a fellow being who would understand the depths of its suffering.

The creature promised again that the two of them would sink deep into the forests where not even those who live in the woods seek shelter, and they would subsist on berries and learn to hunt and eat defenseless woodland creatures that would not be missed. Before I could change my mind again, I consented to my creation's request, spurned from the depths of guilt at having abandoned my only child and out of the sympathy its tale aroused in me.

Once it was satisfied that I was sincere about my agreement, the creature insisted it would return after it was clear this new companion had been made, whether through a typical gestation period as it was conceived or in some other way it expected I had the skills to create. It did not explain how, but it made it clear we would not need to speak again. The monstrosity said that it would watch my movements closely enough to see how I developed this new body for its fulfillment.

Then, just like that, it was gone. I was left holding my head in my hands wishing for a different life, one free from the pain I felt, the responsibility I could not squash. I greatly wished Hana were there, so she could advise me. But I knew if she were, she would probably be filled with her own anger and sadness at how I let this disastrous story wreak so much havoc in our lives and take us so far from the lives we had hoped to share. I took a long walk in the woods that surrounded the small cabin, hoping it would ease the anxiety I now felt at the task before me. But each bird's cry and star in the night sky only furthered my anguish. I felt mocked by their ease; my own existence was so depraved, and yet I only had myself to blame. The next morning, bleary-eyed and disoriented, I drove into town so I could get back into the lab and see what I could make of this insurmountable undertaking.

What happened next was something I could have never predicted. But it would change the course of my life forever.

Dr. Frank went to the guest room to take a nap. I wasn't surprised she was fatigued from telling such a complicated and painful story. I wondered at her constant misgendering of her creature, and if it was a way to create distance between herself and who she had created. So that perhaps it would feel less real. But it struck me as strange and disorienting for a nonbinary person to be unable to hold all the truths that lay within the one she had made. I felt I had circled the entire world since that first day Dr. Wang and I had seen her in such a frazzled state, only a few weeks ago now. It was not just the story that surprised me. It was also her trust in me to share a story so personal and vulnerable. Even though it may seem far-fetched—who would believe such a thing?—I felt in her candor and her gaze upon me as she recalled the most painful parts that it was all too true. Truer than even Dr. Frank wanted to admit.

While Dr. Frank was resting, I walked outside and dialed Dr. Wang's number.

"Dr. Wang, 是我."[33] I uttered just louder than a whisper.

"Yes, yes, 我知道.[34] Is everything all right? How is Dr. F?" she asked casually.

"Listen, you're not going to believe what she has told me," I said, but Dr. Wang interrupted me.

"I don't want to hear a word about it. If she has gained your confidence, that is great news. I knew you were up to the task of helping her figure out how to put whatever is going on behind her. But, please, hold her confidence tight to your chest and use your instincts. It's out of my hands now. I trust you implicitly."

"I understand, Dr. Wang. Thank you for everything."

"Good luck. If you need anything, you know where to find me." And with that, Dr. Wang hung up.

The sun had just begun to set when we took our leave of one another. I was also far more tired from holding Dr. Frank's story for so many hours than I realized. We slept for several hours, deep through the night. In my dreams, Ash visited me, even though we had never met, and I had never laid eyes upon dia before. But Ash was not dressed as Dr. Frank had described, but much more elegantly, with fine linen trousers and well-made leather sandals. Sometimes Ash's long, red hair

---

33 shì wǒ—it's me

34 wǒ zhīdào—I know

fell in soft curls down dia back, sometimes in perfect double braids that the creature brought in front of each shoulder. Ash was shirtless and dia back and chest had clearly been shaved recently, as the skin was a bit raw but completely free of the layer of red hair that Dr. Frank had described on multiple occasions while telling her sordid story. I dreamt of another creature, too, but this one was much younger than I had envisioned during Dr. Frank's recounting of Ash's tale and dia request of her, but she did not have the taut expression of exhaustion and rage that Ash did. Her body was wide and misshapen, but her face held the mark of inner peace I could not relate to. Her hair was of a deep auburn that fell far past her bottom, the way Ma's still appears to me in my dreams, from a memory of so many years ago.

They approached one another, Ash and this smaller, softer creature with a much more feminine embodiment, and held one another for what felt like hours within the world of the dream. I could feel myself smiling through the fantasy my subconscious concocted. But my smile quickly faded. As they held one another, suddenly the smaller creature began to gradually melt as if struck with fire and to shrink in such hideous colors and distortions until she was no longer, and Ash's arms were empty of any flesh. Dia wailed in deep agony, and I could still hear the sound reverberate in my ears as I quaked myself awake, my arms crossed, hands gripping my biceps, trembling in fright.

*

The sweat covering my chest and arms was ice cold, even though it was balmy outside, and my apartment had been cool just hours before. Dr. Frank gently tapped at the door to see if I was all right. I told her I would be right out and tried to compose myself. I did not want to let on that I was so unsettled by her story that my sleep was overtaken by nightmares—I was afraid if it was too obvious how disturbed I was, she would take it personally, or not tell me what happened next. I was riveted, and I wanted to know whether or not she did, indeed, finish her creature's request.

When I came out into the living room, Dr. Frank was sitting on my meager vintage patterned sofa I had found at a local thrift store at the beginning of the internship. Her hands were clasped together, sandwiched between her knees. Her skin was of a paler shade than before, but I wasn't that surprised by the change, as I'm sure to retell such a story must have opened all those old wounds again. But there was something else to her demeanor. I couldn't put my finger on it. I didn't have to wait long to find out.

"If you don't mind, would you finish the story?" I asked delicately, nervously looking in my lap. "Did you end up fulfilling Ash's request? I imagine that must have been a difficult undertaking, to say the least. How did it all turn out?"

Dr. Frank cleared her throat and didn't speak for several minutes, leading my mind down a million possible paths of conclusions and anxieties.

"Actually, that's what I want to talk to you about now."

"Oh?" I tried to respond nonchalantly, but the words caught in my throat, dry mouthed and terrified. What on earth could she mean by that?

"I want to first start off by telling you how much I appreciate your kindness and generosity these past few weeks, and your tender spirit. I can tell that my story had an impact on you, and that means quite a great deal to me," Dr. Frank said.

"Oh, of course. I'm so sorry for all that you've been through," I responded with a smile, unclear of what was ahead.

"The reason I have not been able to fulfill this request is because I have not found a proper surrogate. I have been looking for the right person. As you can imagine, it's not easy to find someone who will treat this situation with the delicate nature it requires. I have been looking for a young person who knows enough about science so I wouldn't have to spend so much time explaining."

I nodded slowly. "Yes, I can only imagine that it would need to be the perfect person."

"Exactly. And that is why, when I have hired interns, I have asked my staff to only hire candidates who are of child-bearing age, and with no . . . what is the appropriate word here . . . attachments that might become complications."

"Mmhmm," I offered, my voice dropping in volume.

"I knew when Dr. Wang told me about you that you were special. I had not one doubt in my mind that you were the perfect person for this . . . what should we call it . . . venture of mine." She smiled then, but her expression was unsettling and disproportionate to where I feared she was leading. I brought my head forward into my lap to stop myself from becoming dizzy.

"Are you all right?" Dr. Frank placed a hand on my back. Her touch thrilled me and made me slightly squeamish all at once. After a few moments, I raised my head back up to meet her gaze.

"Oh yes, I'm okay. This is just a lot. Is this, is this why I was asked to care for you? I mean, it's fine if it is. After all, you're the head of this company. But. Did you set me up? Was what happened to you in the lab a setup?" It was scary to accuse someone I admired so much, who could take away everything I relied on to survive. But I couldn't make sense of all that had transpired to lead us to this point.

"No, no, no, don't be silly. I'm no actor," she laughed, and I giggled half-heartedly. "I have been in such a state because I was losing all hope I would find someone to help me do this. And of course, I just simply have too many duties here to carry the child myself. Besides, I'm much too old now. Too much at stake." I nodded.

"Do you think that you would be up for it? You would learn more about this work in nine short months than you could learn in ten years of research. And, of course, I would quickly teach you all that I have learned over the course of my life so that you could proceed with any position you could dream of in this field. I would recommend you for whatever lab you seek to work under. Mine would obviously be available for the taking, if that is what you desire. Up to you."

I couldn't help but hear her words echo the story she had told me, how she said the same thing to Ezra before rejecting his marriage proposal. It was odd and disorienting to suddenly be thrusted from listener of a story to participant.

Being asked to carry Ash's companion was such a shock that my mouth dropped open, my breath caught in my stomach. If the situation had shifted only ever so slightly, this moment would have been what I dreamed of. But instead, it was more like a dream and a nightmare intertwined, like lovers or the trickiest sort of enemies.

"I know it's a lot to ask. I understand if you don't feel comfortable to embark on this with me. Of course, it would require your absolute confidence, your most thorough work. You would not be able to tell Dr. Wang or any of the other workers in the lab. I think it could perhaps be something very exciting for you, if you are able to contend with the facts around it." I swallowed audibly, and then smiled to hide how nervous I was.

"I know you aren't aware of this, but I've been studying your work in the lab for some time, and so, yes, you're right in the sense that it wasn't an accident that I would end up here recovering from my terrible tragedy with you as my nurse, so to speak. I'm also aware that I've already warned you against being too fixated on the progress of ambition. But this is the last step in a long and terrible journey, and I am hoping you will help me finish it, forever. I suppose ambition is an impossible thing to give up completely, no matter the cost."

I swallowed again, perhaps a little too loudly this time,

and ran my hand anxiously through my hair. She gingerly touched my knee, which bounced against the short coffee table. I started to attempt, awkwardly, to speak.

"Please, don't feel you have to answer now. But it would give you the opportunity to work with all the techniques you've been kept from. We're the only lab in the States that's willing to work with IVG. Could be pretty life-changing for you, and for your career from here, wherever you decide to go next. Just think about it."

Before I could utter a word in response Dr. Frank slipped out of the room and retired for the rest of the day and night.

And then, the story started wriggling around like a snake, one you think you can befriend, saying to yourself, perhaps this snake isn't like all the others, or perhaps, just perhaps, our thoughts on these creatures all come from our own wretched perspective, and maybe they aren't as monstrous as we imagine them to be.

At first, the work together was incredibly exciting. My pulse raced from the opportunity—here I was, this little plum from the forest, getting the chance to work with the top scientist in my field. Just moments ago, I was a lowly intern, a gofer logging in samples and studies. Like a small child trying to reach the shoulders of the great giants who surrounded me, doing all the important work. But, having come from the streets, having lost my Ko, and believing I wouldn't make it, that I would end up lost to the forest as so many had been, this was quite something compared to how I imagined I would meet my end. I had a roof over my head, enough money to buy frozen dumplings and ingredients for a decent stir-fry every day, and tea to keep me going through the long hours of work each night. I had no family, no great love of my life, but I had long ago made my peace with my solitude.

Most days that I worked with Dr. Frank, I couldn't quite believe my own eyes. The work was very complex, actually, and we spent weeks and weeks calculating everything. Dr. Frank showed me her video archives of the early experiments with the pygmy tarsiers, the early stages of Hana's pregnancy. It was only after she showed me the videos of Hana that Dr. Frank admitted to me that she had snuck into the hospital after Hana died and stolen preserved tissue from Hana. She had it frozen in the lab for future use. If she had to go about this again, maybe she could at least go about it in the right way. In those early days, Dr. Frank told me she imagined they would make multiple children together, and even if Hana wouldn't always be the surrogate for these experiments, she had hoped Hana wouldn't mind using her own materiality so Dr. Frank could perfect this ongoing search for how to make the perfect child.

I did question whether it was a good idea for Dr. Frank to use the material from someone who meant so much to her, who brought such associations with the deepest forms of loss. Would it make it difficult for Dr. Frank to relinquish this new child to Ash? Given that Hana most likely did not carry the genetic mutation that caused Ash's disability, would it be more difficult for Ash to attach to this child? Would this be what Ash wanted? But what did I know compared to Dr. Frank? It wasn't my place to say. I was just thrilled to have a seat at the table.

We didn't spend all of our time working. When the weather was nice, Dr. Frank would surprise me, out of the blue, and pull me swinging out of my chair, a kind of intimacy that made the hairs on my arms dance, and take us out for a canoe ride on a nearby lake or suggest I accompany her on an impromptu picnic at a city park. These moments were a much-needed break from the grueling hours of study and the harsh neon light of the lab.

But, looking back now, I can see those outings were meant to blur my surroundings with such confusion, too, such excitement. During one picnic, I looked up after fixing a slice of cheese on a wheat cracker only to catch Dr. Frank's gaze steadfastly directed at me.

"Yes, Dr. F?" I inquired sheepishly, unsure of how to respond to such a change in the pulse of our dynamic after we had already embarked on this new, more electrifying project together, one rife with risk and drama.

The corners of her mouth turned up, ever so slightly. I couldn't help but be taken in by her, the largeness of her and what she meant to me, by the attention she deigned to give to someone as small and unworthy as me. Such a sensitive story, one that could certainly threaten her career, and yet, it was me she chose for this mission, me she trusted with this confidence. As if all of the worth and importance of my entire life was wrapped up in the package of Dr. Frank alone.

"Please, call me Z. Or, anything you like, really. Just don't call me something so formal as Doctor, not when we are making such important, and intimate, work together." My hand trembled behind hers, which made her clasp mine even more firmly and made the sigh within my chest mirror the quickening shudder of my hand.

"Uh, okay, Z," I nervously offered back as an attempt, trying to appear calm. I knew it wasn't working.

"Is everything okay?" I tried to get at what was behind her gaze, which had intensified. I also didn't want to assume there was anything more behind it.

"Oh yes, darling," she smiled again, her voice smooth as brandy.

"I just like to look at you, if you don't mind?" With that, she placed a hand on my cheek. I was instantly a goner, taken with her in a completely different way than I was with Ko. I felt out of control of myself but also incredibly filled with the magnitude of what it meant for Dr. F to touch me. There was some part of me that felt this was all too much, too fast, too wild, too messy, too irrational. But I was alone. There was no one to witness the recklessness of what I was starting to surrender to with Dr. Frank. I imagine that even if there was, I would have been too swept up by its power to listen.

We fell back on the blanket, and I let her take me, having no understanding what, exactly, of myself I was consenting to give.

I fell further and further down the hole of work with Z. The closer we came to reaching our goal, the more agitated she became. What caused her so much worry, I could tell, even though she would not say it out loud to me, even when I asked, was correcting Ezra's mistakes while still making this experiment a viable companion for Ash.

I could feel Ash hovering around us—sometimes, when I imagined Ash wasn't expecting anyone to pay attention, if I jerked my eye quickly enough, I saw the dark shadow of dia loom large from a sliver of the window's reflection. I often wondered what Ash thought of me, how much dia really observed of our new connection. When we took our breaks from the lab, Z felt like a dream I hoped to never wake from. A presence that threatened to consume, an attentiveness I didn't think was possible, so rapturous it felt laced with something else, like a poison too powerful for me to understand or come to terms with. But when we returned to the lab and to our separate workspaces, she felt like a different person—one whose rage was murderous if I made a miscalculation or gave her an answer she wasn't satisfied with. That didn't mean the answer was wrong, necessarily; only that she was hoping for something other than what I had resolved of this problem or that one.

I hate to admit it, but sometimes, even in our lovemaking, so raw I felt our bodies apart from it, I desperately missed Ko. I wondered what she was doing out there in the world without me, without us. Did she miss me, too? I missed her imperfections and her kindnesses, the simplicity of how we loved one another, her inexplicable magic. But I was so deep into this new life, I couldn't imagine returning to that old life. I didn't know the who I would be that would return to it.

For the most part, I was too enthralled with Z to push back on any of her troubling behaviors—I accepted her disorienting shifts from her overly affectionate ways and her inflexible rages. I supposed I had been groomed from the start, with an absent mother and a terrifying father, to take whatever it was Z would give me. But what I found surprising in myself was one of the few times I provoked Z with my own expression of anger, which had to do with her constant misgendering of Ash.

I can't recall what it was we were discussing when she referred to Ash as *it*, a choice I assumed she made intentionally.

"Z, please. You told me yourself Ash's pronoun is dia," I said, at first meekly, shy to question someone so large and important as Z when I felt so small.

Z was silent for what felt like much longer than a minute

or two. She turned her entire body to face me, peering at me over her glasses. It was a move I recognized but one I hadn't identified until then. A move my father would choreograph into his body to demonstrate his anger. My realization of this parallel took the breath out of my chest.

"Are you serious?" Z asked finally, a haughty smirk, which repulsed me, crossing her face. At that moment, I wanted to take back any decision I had made to cross the boundary of obedient pupil to equal. Even as our bodies had crossed those boundaries and intertwined with one another, we would never be the same.

"I didn't mean anything by it." My voice shook. I sat on my hands, so Z couldn't see them tremble. "I find it striking that you would continue to misgender Ash when you, yourself, identify as a masculine woman, as a calalai. Don't you see it's a place where you meet in the middle, share a common experience?"

I didn't hear the lab stool creak or even see her move. Suddenly, she was upon me, her face inches from mine, so close I could see her exposed pores. Her breath was hot against my face, sickeningly sweet.

"You are here, my child," she began, and what seemed inspiring and powerful before now felt menacing, "because I have allowed you to be. Don't think for a second you know the first thing about what I have made or what I am made of. How dare you compare me to that curse? Just sit back and wait until I tell you what to do. And when it's time, care for the pregnancy until you are ready to deliver. Otherwise, don't utter a single word. Understand?"

I nodded, but only so she would ease away from me. I saw Z for what she was then, and I felt within my whole body what she had done to Ash. It was a gift, really, that she had left dia to the elements. God knows what would have happened if she had somehow wanted Ash for herself. I knew what it was to chase after that withholding parent. It was at that moment I realized I had always been made of more Ash than Z, more creature than scientist.

*

It was soon time to choose when to implant the embryo into my uterus. I was afraid to ask Z when she planned to prepare my body to do this. Ever since the day I approached her about misgendering Ash, the slightest question would set her off. I knew it was the riskiest part of this whole venture. How would we medically embark on this journey as safely as possible given what happened to Hana? I knew at some point these numbers and words and figures and charts had to be turned into actual human life. Did she even remember this was for Ash, that this life had to feel and look and move as dia did? But, ultimately, I didn't feel these curiosities were my business, so I held them tight against me, waiting for her to tell us when the big move would take place.

On the final night of our work together, we barely made it back to my apartment with our eyes open. We shuffled our feet, bleary-eyed and exhausted, back to the larger of the two bedrooms, where we had slept together nightly since beginning to make this new creature for her old one, and collapsed against one another, fully clothed. Just a pile of limbs indistinguishable from one another. And then we slept.

We slept for hours and hours. The sound of Z's breathing comforted me, steady and even for the first time since we had met, her hand stroking the part of my belly exposed from my shirt, which had risen during the early morning shifting that happens during sleep. It was a tenderness I hadn't witnessed from her in quite some time, and I took any inch of tenderness from her that I could grasp.

The harsh southern sun finally woke me. I had no sense of how long I had slept, but I could feel the sweat gathering under my breasts and between my thighs, its stickiness telling me how late into the day it had become. When I opened my eyes, I saw Z had clearly been awake for a while, watching me sleep. She wasn't angry, but something in her had shifted. Something significant.

"Hi, darling," she reached over to massage the fade at the back of my neck.

"You slept for some time, but I didn't mind. I enjoyed watching you. Your sleep feels like the rhythm of an ocean wave." She smiled, tugging on my earlobe.

"Oh, I think I slept off all of the work we've been doing since the beginning. I felt like I could have slept forever," I yawned, trying to shift the mood I sensed approaching me. I was still too disoriented to predict the next bombshell. Her touch was sweet but it accompanied something I couldn't quite reach.

"I have an idea for you, an incredible opportunity depending on how you choose to look at it," she continued, scattering little kisses from my fingertips up the back of my hand, then my arm, my shoulder, my neck, and down my back.

It was impossible to concentrate on what she was saying. She was a storm I couldn't ignore, lilting and soft, but with the potential to rage against the roof and all that was held secure at any moment.

"Mmhmm," I responded, but I wasn't really listening.

As she continued to tend to me in ways that filled me with excitement and provoked a sudden and intense desire in me for another body, that wasn't Ko's, she asked me if I was now ready to be the surrogate for her and Hana's creation. But not as originally planned. To share a child with her, to be partners in this work together. She was convinced this time it would turn out all right, and perhaps, she whispered in my ear in a manner that made my entire body slack, we wouldn't have to give the child away this time.

I knew what she was asking. This time, it wouldn't be Ezra to sabotage the mission. It would be her to sabotage Ash's mission, and to try, yet again, to make the creature Z had always dreamed of.

Maybe it was from the space between me and all those I loved—Ba and Ko, Ma—but whatever the case, I fell for the fantasy I wanted this to become. The shifting tectonic plates in my brain rearranged to take on the look of what I wanted love and family and wholeness to look like.

Who was there, anywhere, to argue with me?

李

How can I describe what it was like to carry this child, connected to a future I knew from the start was never mine?

On a good day, the world spread out in front of me like a vast plain. Who knew what lay hidden beneath the roots, what would spring forth from the earth in due time? In those days, Z was tender and patient with me and brought me nourishment. She found me increasingly appealing, no doubt from all that my belly was providing for her future progress and at worst, because I was an end to the disaster she'd been living with alone for such a long time. I didn't tell Z this, but sometimes I would lie in bed with a hand on my belly, and as the creature inside me pushed against my stomach, beat-beat, pulse-pulse, I thought of what life I could offer them. I thought of Ma, and how, if I had my choice, I would most definitely never leave this wondrous pulse of flesh talking to me from deep inside my body. I thought of Ba, and I hoped, if given the chance, that I, as a parent, would always listen. But those days did not last long, as logic would eventually settle in, and I would remember this child was never mine. This child was never Ash's, either, even though it was under the guise of dia desire that this was made. It was always Z's. Everything had been.

As the days settled into weeks, as we traced the seasons passing through my skin while this new little seedling stretched my belly farther and farther outward, I grew more attached to the little body within my body, the little piece of Z's childhood love, which had no choice but to be marked with an imprint of her tragic end. I thought of all the parts of the story my womb now contained within it: Ezra and Hana, and Ash and Pine, and Caroline and even baby Justin, Ezra's small child, lost to Ash's rage over being left. I, too, knew something of the rage of being left behind. And also, throbbing on the inside, I felt Ba, and Ma, and Ko, and all of those old dreams that felt so far from me now.

Carrying a child was never something I dreamed of for myself. When I was deep in the throes of young love with Ko, it was always her body I saw in my fantasies, full and weighted with child after going to the local sperm bank, or sometimes I thought, maybe we would have a nice gay best friend who would donate his sperm, or even raise the child alongside us. Someone like Hunter, maybe, or another kind spirit we would have met along the way in the forest who had aspirations of getting beyond it one day.

Although at times I deeply doubted the decision I had made in the heat of the moment, influenced by Z's powerful ability to convince me, for the most part, those days were a blur of hormones as my brain swam in a fog of cotton candy and sun, telling me that no matter what, everything would be all right. I was a scientist, after all, and I knew those feelings weren't real. They were the messages the body gave me so that I stayed calm enough for the growth inside me to remain healthy. But, at the end of it, it was just easier to be lulled along on the canoe of ease and to let all the worries sit somewhere else, until I had no choice but to confront them head-on.

I knew I would eventually be forced to face what was on the other side. The shadow, black and menacing in the rearview mirror of each day we spent in Z's house together, which Z insisted we move to while waiting for the little creature to be born, told me so.

李

I hated my breasts during pregnancy. They felt like water balloons bouncing against my chest when I walked. I missed when they were small enough I never thought about them, forgetting they were there unless Z touched them. As the pregnancy progressed, Z knew better than to put her hands on them, even in an act of tenderness or intimacy. She tried to be delicate with my body during those days, to give me some ounce of pleasure that would ease the extraordinary toll this entire undertaking placed on me and my body. As my body wrestled against me, as I wrestled against what I was responsible for putting it through, a consequence of the reckless decision I had made, I started losing an understanding of just what or who I decided to do this for, for someone barely more than a stranger.

I wanted to hold my belly away from the world, make it disappear.

I wanted to take the little body tucked inside it, making

itself known to me, changing my control over it, and run into the woods and hide, so even Z wouldn't find me. But I knew this was a lost cause. I was the one with the least amount of agency in the story. I knew either Z or Ash would always find us. If I held my belly away from the world, could I keep the little heart beating inside me safe?

What did I know of safety? Who was there to teach me?

The body inside me started to grow exponentially, as we knew it would, as it had to, so that Ash would feel we were doing our best to fulfill the mission at hand, to give dia a companion that felt like Ash without risking my life during childbirth. Ash did not know Z had no intention of making their second creature one similar to dia, or that Z would never give this child up. So as this creature grew, my belly expectantly grew in traditional ways. I only hoped Z and Hana did not share any genetic mutations they did not know about. I found it perplexing Z would not have taken care of these tests already, but she seemed insistent Ezra's genetic mutation had been an aberration. It was a sign, she said, that the universe had never wanted him to have a child to begin with. I knew this was not my battle, so when Z spoke this way, I remained silent. As my body expanded to allow room for this new creature, my belly reminded me of blocks of clay, haphazard and lumpy before I beat them with the heel of my palms to obey my hands. But, of course, the body wasn't a lump of clay. If I beat my belly into submission, I could end up squashing the little growing clay inside, bleeding out from within. I was afraid to test just how little Z cared for me in earnest, how much I was merely a vessel to give her what she wanted. The truth was, I knew the answer all along. I just didn't want to face it. It was another Ma, discarding me once I proved no longer useful. If she wanted the child bruising my skin with its strength and stunning size, Z would have to pry it from my arms.

I kept myself and the little purr inside of me alive by indulging in dreams of Z that would never come to light: The two of us splashed across the front pages of the latest science magazines or popping up on everyone's latest social media feed, people knowing we'd changed embryology research forever. Hand in hand, walking into an award ceremony, being jointly honored. Or, sometimes, that fantasy would be replaced with one where she won the most distinctive honor, her gratitude focused only on me, how she couldn't imagine where she would be without my steady love and support to guide her through.

The dreams didn't always orbit ambition, but they did often, because that's what kept me there longest, pursuing a reputation I hoped would make me feel worthy enough. It didn't occur to me at the time to consider that even my dreams only spun around Z's ambition and progress, never mine. I was always the accompaniment, the support behind the great mind, like a woman behind a man. I was never another like-minded genius, standing alongside her, pursuing my own work, my own genius.

Maybe I pursued this world of medical science not quite a doctor like Ba, but orbiting the world where Ba spent so many nights away from me, only to feel closer to him. Despite the welts he branded into my body's memory, he was still the only family I had ever known, the only one who had never left me. He was the only one I chose to leave instead. But, if you ask me, that wasn't really a choice I made, but one that had been made for me so long ago, since the first time Ba left marks on my legs when I was the age of little Justin who didn't make it.

As my brain tried to make sense of the body that thumped against my stomach to be heard, I had other dreams. Dreams of Ba, visions of him holding the infant I knew would never materialize, one formed the way it was supposed to, with proportionate traits and a face Ba would coo at. A partner Ba would accept with open arms, whose Asianness he would see as a bridge between us. But this was a dream that brought too much pain, because even in my fantasies I knew it would never come true.

While Z spent more time in the lab, hiding out from the future so soon to be thrust upon us in a place no longer safe for me or the infant we were building together, I tried to focus on the truth of our story. A story that would end with my making it through to the other side, where the child we birthed into the world would be loved by Ash. A story that would end with two monsters, orphaned and abandoned, caring for one another, set against the world that threatened to tear it asunder.

I tried not to think of Hana's tale of obliteration and blood, a body she agreed to carry that only became the death of her instead, that consumed her very flesh with its size and disproportion. Did Z make the right calculations so I could live, so that this child might be a little bit less miserable than the one she'd made before? Would I become another casualty of Z's pride and wanting? What about my wants? Would I find room in this body, among Z's wants and Ash's needs, among the child that needed my blood and skin to survive, for my own yearning and sanctuary?

李

O what can I say of what came next?

Z was never someone I would consider warm or particularly nurturing, but I suppose you only truly learn how giving one's nature is when the moment is forced upon them. Certainly, the way we came to one another was so strange and unorthodox it's not as though I waited to discover her true nature before making a decision that would brand us together for eternity.

I had no model, anyway, for what the gaze of love looked like. Looking back now, I realize that a piece of my heart died when Ko left me. In my mind, she deserted me to die, knowing I would be on the streets alone, deserted to the dangerous whims of nature and men. I wonder still, did she find someone else to hold her secrets? Or did she let that part of her die along with us, hidden in the rustling wind that gossiped with the trees we exploited for our shelter? It was too painful to think about. I had enough pain to occupy my mind with.

I thought Z would care for me the further along in pregnancy I became. That, at some point, while I spent day and night in bed, my legs and head elevated by pillows, my large, misshapen belly casting frightening oblong shadows on the wall, Z would nourish me with her mother's Indonesian recipes she spoke of at length when she was in a nostalgic mood, or rub my belly with Tiger Balm when I became itchy and marked with discomfort. That, even though this child was not meant to be ours, she would place her smooth palm against my skin as the child kicked a stampede into the lining of my stomach, and smile at me the way I had seen couples smile at one another in the movies.

No hand graced my belly when it kicked. No tray of food was left waiting for me while I slept. No smile.

If any change arose in the Creator of the growing thing incubating inside of me, it was that Z spent even more time away from us. I didn't know what experiment she was investigating at all hours of the night, what question she was desperate to answer. But the longer the hours of nothingness and silence in the apartment continued, the more frightened I became of what was to follow. I could feel the child preparing its exit, and although I found pregnancy scary and lonely and disconcerting, and incredibly uncomfortable, I felt something else grow. A protectiveness over my belly, which now teemed with a little life, but one that loomed large. As long as the creation within me stayed inside, I could keep it safe—not only from Ash, who felt wild and untenable, but also from Z, whose rage and grief seemed a terrifying combination. I also knew, as long as the infant could stay within my depths, I, too, could manage to stay alive on its behalf. At least, I took Hana's surviving through to the end of her pregnancy as a good sign for my own livelihood.

I knew this was ultimately a foolish wish, a reckless desire. I knew that human life required the air outside of skin and fluid and nutrients beyond the parasitic pairing of gestational consumption.

If only I had a partner that could soothe me out of such paranoias. Z was no such partner. I was alone, preparing to birth a child I had no claim over. I was just a vessel to serve a purpose. After the half-Hana, half-Z creature was born, it's not as though I could go back to working at the lab. Where would I go then? Just like Ash, I was floating through the world, desperate to find a ground to root myself to.

And then, I had an idea. I knew just when and how to execute it.

I was eight months pregnant by that point, and the anxiety and isolation I felt about my particular circumstances made me even more insistent on what I felt I must do.

It had been months since I had opened my computer. I had become too large and unwieldy to work on much of anything. I couldn't remember the last time I worked on my own studies or anything connected to my own life.

I opened up a new document on my computer and began to type a letter to Ko. There was too much to say. It would take an entire novel's worth of words to let her know everything that had happened since we last parted. Besides, I had no time. That would take hours I didn't have. I decided to try something simpler.

Dearest Ko—

I don't know how this letter will reach you, if you have moved on from us in all the years that have passed since we last spoke. Perhaps you have a new partner now, children of your own you care for with the tenderness I remember so vividly. I hope you have been happy. I miss you so much, but I have never quite known how to reach out to you, what to say. And although I do hope there will be time for us to share with each other all that's happened since that cold, dark night so long ago, I don't have time for that now. Let me explain, as I need you more than I have ever needed anyone.

It is a long story, one I can tell you in time. But, I'm due to give birth in a few weeks, and I'm in a very compromised position. I feel the person I agreed to carry this child for is dangerous and does not have the best interests of me or the child in mind.

I'm going to leave you my address where you can reach me, and a time frame when I'll be alone. Is it possible you could help me? I call on you in desperation, love, and urgency that my child will not face the life I and so many others have. If I do not leave before the child's birth, I'm afraid of what will happen to me and to this vulnerable child. It's too much to get into now, but I hope you can take my word for it.

All my love,
your Plum

Before Z returned home from working her late hours at the lab, I quickly printed out the letter for Ko and I stuffed it into an envelope with an address I found on the computer that I hoped was current and walked it across the street to feed it into a standing mailbox. I crossed all my fingers with my eyes closed, took a deep breath, and waddled back to the house in my flip-flops, the only shoes that still fit my swollen feet, and eased my unwieldy body back onto my bed, and waited.

李

How can I describe the birth? I suppose it is something to say I am still here to tell the story.

But, I should start before that. With Ko.

I had given up hope on Ko. Perhaps the letter had never reached her, I reasoned. Perhaps the address was outdated, or, even worse, Ko had a whole new wondrous, enriching life, one I would only make more complicated with my reckless decisions that landed me in this mess. As each day swam into the next, I tried to banish all the scenarios from my mind. It did no good anyway. The best thing to do was prepare myself for the birth and for whatever would happen afterwards.

And then, just two weeks before my due date, I heard a rapping at the door. I jumped at the sound of it. I assumed it was Ash, coming to make dia presence known. But it wasn't. It was Ko. Ko, Ko, Ko, Ko. She had come to rescue me. She was my savior all along.

I managed to heave my body off of the bed and, leaning

on the walls for support, slowly made my way over to the backdoor, which had a square of glass cut into its center. Ko peered through the glass, her hand cupped around her face, but the light was too harsh to see anything through it. She began to call for me: "Plum, are you there? It's me, darling! Please open the door. Are you okay?"

I grabbed my set of keys from a small basket in the living room and frantically tried to open the door, but my hands were so swollen, and I was so nervous that I dropped the keys on the floor twice. After considerable effort, I finally got the door open, and there she was. There was my Ko. Her hair was shorter and her clothes were more formal, but they still possessed a sense of the tender personality I remembered. Her expression, soft and forthright, her soft, full lips, her eyes, they were all just as I remembered. I fell into her, and we both cried for what felt like hours.

Ko was the one to break us from our reunion.

"Darling, hi," she beamed at me. "I have so many things I want to say, and I'm sure you do, too. But," she began, as she took in the full sight of my pregnant body, standing awkwardly over the threshold of Z's backdoor, "right now, we have to get you out of here. I'm so sorry it took me so long," Ko said hurriedly, rushing into the house to find my things.

"I can't tell you what it is for me to see you right now," I said, standing at the threshold, taking her in. Ko, my darling Ko, standing in the house of this sordid tale and disaster I had allowed myself to become part of. She looked back at me and smiled.

"Whatever it is for you, I promise, plum tree, it is the same for me. But, right now, let's get your things. I don't want her to come in while we're here. What a mess that would be. Are you packed somewhere? Maybe you had a bag for the hospital if I wasn't able to come for you?" She walked back over to me and put her hand on my cheek. I melted, wobbling on my feet.

"Oh, it's in the back closet in the guest room, behind all the clothes." I started to walk towards the spare room with her, the one I imagined Hana had spent just as many lost and lonely nights in as I had.

"No, darling, please. You sit. I'll take care of everything. Once I load the car, I'll come back for you," she said, rushing into the room. Ko grabbed some drinks and snacks from the fridge and pantry in Z's kitchen. She worked fast, and before long, we were on the road, headed back to wherever it was that Ko lived. I didn't care where it was. All I knew was I was out of Z's reach, and I was with Ko, and that the creature growing inside of me would be safe.

*

To be honest, I don't remember much of the labor itself, but I recall that just as I was beginning prelabor complications, Ko placed a hot cloth on my forehead. I couldn't believe how differently this moment was turning out to be from what I had originally imagined. I shuddered at the thought and then banished it from my mind.

I was too sedated to be able to remember it all. Our child

was larger than a traditional child, but she was born healthy, without the complications of Ash's birth. Oftentimes near the end of my pregnancy, I wondered what Ash was doing, if dia was still alive. Would Ash really make Z's life miserable after not receiving the creature dia requested? Even now, I can still feel the deep wounding of the incision across my belly. Sometimes I trace the scar the procedure left, as it's all I have to remind me of that time.

On one side of me was Ko, coaxing me through the birth as I fell in and out of consciousness from the pain and drugs Silber administered. After discussing it at length with Ko, telling Ko everything that transpired with Z and all that Z told me, we decided it made the most sense to have Silber with us as a support for the delivery, a note of gratitude for all she had done for Hana. Besides, this was Hana's biological child. In a sense, it was the child Hana was always meant to have.

Just before the birth, I sent Silber a very long letter of everything that had happened. She responded quickly, thanking me for my confidence, and saying that nothing would please her more than to support us. Silber lived with us those few days before the birth and for a few weeks after. We spent many hours commiserating over Z's narcissistic ways and how enraging her pattern of withholding from Hana was. I could tell Silber cared deeply for Hana. Ko and I often wondered if anything more happened between them, but we never pried further. At the final hour of the delivery, just before Silber sedated me so she could cut me open to remove the creation Z urged me to fulfill for her, I begged Ko to name her myself.

"I know we will raise this child as our own. But, after all that I've been through, I just really want to be the one to name the little pea," I whined, wailing through tears, reminding me of how I used to scream my needs, at long last, to Ba, knowing that quieting my tears and cries was the only way he would ever acquiesce to my desires.

"Z seduced me into being her container for this experiment. As soon as she got what she wanted, I became empty to her. Like paper," I moaned.

"Shh, shh," Ko soothed in my ear, bringing me out of my fever dream. "Of course you can name the plumlet," she winked. I smiled through the pain as her voice reminded me of an earlier time filled with fantasy and potential. Maybe now that I was with Ko, it could be that again.

"Whatever you would like." She placed a hand on my belly then. It had a mothering effect on me, and I closed my eyes.

"But, darling," she said, searching my face for a sign, "you know this child can never be ours, right? It will always be dia," she gestured her head out the window, where beyond the bright wash of light we imagined Ash loomed, ready to take the very thing that returned us to one another, even though we knew Ash had no idea where we were, so far from Z and anything Ash knew.

I knew this question, and this fate, would come. I had known it from the first moment Z told me her story. And yet, it was more than I could stomach. I began to weep a deep, body-heaving cry that made the medical bed under me shake from the weight of us. I wept for all the losses of my still young life—for Ba, and Ma, and Z, and the life I dreamt I would have with my creation, a creation that was never mine, but only of me.

Ko stroked my hair as I wept.

As my crying subsided, Ko offered that we could think about what to do about Ash later, and asked me a final question, just before the next dose of liquid sedative hit my bloodstream.

"Well, then. Darling, what would you like to name our unwieldy little creature?" Ko smiled.

I did not hesitate.

"Iphis," I told her. I did not tell Ko why. I didn't have to. Iphis was the story of the girl raised as a boy after her father threatened to kill any child of her mother's that was anything but male. The girl raised as a boy who fell in love with a girl, and was only able to marry her after the Egyptian goddess Isis, moved by her story of love and disguise, transformed her into a boy. It was a story Ko shared with me one day during one of those late nights at the ceramics studio, just before our first kiss. I infused my child that I made with Z with the love I had for Ko. I hoped that wherever Iphis ended up, she would be happy and well cared for and that through Ash's experience of love from Pine, intertwined with a knowing of loss and abandonment from Z, she would find solace and attachment. I wanted her to have something more than I had, something more than I was allowed to offer her myself.

It was in this state of blessing the child that wasn't to be mine that I fell into the deepest sleep.

EPILOGUE

"Iphis! Ash! Ko! It's time!" 李 called from where she sat on the floor next to the sofa, holding a volume of papers simply bound with a metal wire coil in her hand.

Iphis bounded down the stairs vigorously, loud enough the coffee table shook from where it rested in front of the sofa against the bamboo floors. By the time Iphis made it to the living room, Ko was sitting on the sofa next to 李, stroking her hand. Ash stood next to 李, smiling down at her. Iphis ran over to Ko and nestled her head onto her chest. Ko kissed her delicately on the top of her forehead.

"So, I'm dying to know. Ma Plum, what exactly is this surprise I've had to wait all my life for anyway? Are you actually going to give this to me now? Really?" Iphis asked as Ko poked her in the rib. Iphis giggled, a bell of a laugh that made 李 smile.

"Darling," 李 began, standing up next to Ash. "You know Mama Ko and I have always done things differently than your friends you've gone to school with, and that's not just because we're Americans," 李 winked at Ko. "It's because our family has a special origin story, but one you wouldn't be able to understand properly until you were old enough."

"Mmhmm, intrigued. I'm listening," Iphis said, nestling further into Ko, who whispered sternly at her to pay attention. Iphis sat up and leaned forward, resting her elbows on her knees.

"And you know we moved to Indonesia because that is where one of your birthparents is from; well, two, if you count Bissu Ash here, and because, ironically, sometimes you have to go to the source to leave it," 李 said, smirking at Ash and Ko.

Iphis looked ahead of her then, to the wooden deck, the large windows that overlooked the bay, the palm trees and tropical greenery and white orchids that encircled their house. She smiled.

"Okay, okay, curious, but still confused. So, you're about to tell me my story?" Iphis's eyes grew large and expansive. 李 giggled.

"Well, we're not going to tell you the story. That would be too hard to get right. But Bissu Ash is going to *read* you *the* story, which contains in it all of our stories. And your story, too. Get ready for a long night, darling." 李 smiled and sat back down. Iphis's smile grew larger than her face then, and she leaned back into Ko, who stroked her hair.

"Ash, shall I let you take it away then? Oh, and one more thing. Happy eighteenth birthday, sweet creature of mine. What a gift you are to all of us." 李 reached over and grabbed a mooncake from a dish in front of her. Ash, Ko, and Iphis followed suit, clinking mooncakes like champagne glasses.

Ash cleared dia throat.

"I will probably butcher the Mandarin scattered throughout, but I've been practicing since you were born, so I hope I do it justice," Ash said, smiling at 李.

"Here goes nothing," Ash cleared dia throat one last time.

Like all stories, this story starts with a secret, my darkest one. It is not necessary that the secret I held so close to my chest is the darkest one for the world, only that it is so in my heart.

我叫李.[35] If you do not read or understand Mandarin, just Plum will do. At least, that's what Ko called me. And it's the only name that matters to me now. But it is also our family's name, one we share with 李小龍. [36] He is someone who has always mattered a great deal to me, since we are both caught between two worlds. We both share Chinese fathers and mothers from the paperwhites, a connection I grew to understand is rarer than expected.

This is a story of ambition gone wrong. I was warned, and then warned again, and yet, it didn't stop me. 可是[37] maybe my story will help you, even in some small way. At least it's my wish that it will help another not stray so far from what matters. Someone once told me the only way to move on from something is to go through it. By the time I realized how true this was, it was too late for me. I only hope that this letter gets to you in time.

---

35 Wǒ jiào Lǐ—I'm called Lǐ. (Lǐ is a common surname but also translates to plum.)

36 Lǐ Xiǎolóng—Bruce Lee

37 kěshì—but

Notes

Shelley, Mary Wollstonecraft. *Frankenstein; or, The modern Prometheus.* London, Printed for Lackington, Hughes, Harding, Mavor, & Jones, 1818. Pdf. https://www.loc.

Acknowledgments

In one way or another, this book has been brewing in me for over half my life, since I first read Mary Shelley's *Frankenstein* as a sophomore in college. I am most indebted to her and the world she created that hasn't let go of me since.

I began this novel at, ironically (or not, depending on how you look at it) Mary Shelley Month: A Laboratory for Fiction, a writers-in-residence program which attempted to foster a set of conditions similar to those Mary Shelley found herself in when she first wrote the story of Victor Frankenstein's Creature coming to life. I'm incredibly grateful for "a room of one's own" in which to write at The Wellstone Center in the Redwoods. I'm especially grateful to Steve Kettman and Sarah Ringler for their insights, nourishment, and generosity.

There are many writers (and others) along the way who read earlier drafts of the novel, in whole or in part, and whose thoughtful dialogue helped me form what the book would become: Addie Levinsky, Wallace Baine, Mary-Antoinette Smith, Stella Faustino, Tanen Jones, Mariah Stovall, Genevieve Gagne-Hawes, Cassie Mannes Murray, Jen St. Jude, Jess Gherkin, Katie Jean Shinkle, Jas Hammonds, and so many others.

Thank you to my acquisitions editor at Jaded Ibis Press, Lisa Pegram, who immediately understood my vision without question, and who wasn't afraid to love on this book. I'm so thankful to you, in more ways than I can adequately express.

Thank you to my content editors: Shenwei Chang for feedback and edits regarding the Chinese characters & pinyin, and Nadhira Satria, for the scenes and material that emerged from Indonesian and Javanese culture. You both taught me so much.

Thank you to *Room*, *Hearth & Coffin* and *Lambda Literary*, for publishing earlier excerpts from *Unwieldy Creatures.*

When I began *Unwieldy Creatures,* I was in a marriage I believed could make it through, and just days from embarking on my own journey to create a child through reproductive technologies. It was from that impending future I began to question what a Frankenstein might look like in today's futuristic landscape. I birthed this book just before my world fell apart (and just before our entire world changed forever), and somehow managed to finish it after a devastating divorce, amid a quarantine during a raging pandemic. Although that journey would not come to fruition, I was able to rely on my own chosen family, whose love and support I could not have made this book without: TC Tolbert, Zeyn Joukhadar, Piper J. Daniels, Kay Ulanday Barrett, Jas Hammonds, Sarah Sheppeck, Simone Person, Pallavi Govindnathan, Jonathan Caouette, Joseph Osmundson, Angela Peñaredondo, Antonius Bui, Muriel Leung,

Melanie Pang, Ronaldo Wilson, Jo Davis-McElligatt, Sam Ace, Thomas Ayers, John Murphy, Arvin Ramgoolam, and so many others. Please forgive my unreliable memory. I love you all.

& finally, thank you to Jennifer Elkins, without whom this creature could never have taken shape.

Reading List

Ackroyd, Peter. The Casebook of Victor Frankenstein. Anchor Books.

Feder, Rachel. Harvester of Hearts: Motherhood Under the Sign of Frankenstein. Northwestern University Press.

Fisch, Audrey A, Anne K. Mellor, and Esther H. Schor, eds. The Other Mary Shelley: Beyond Frankenstein. Oxford University Press.

Gordon, Charlotte. Romantic Outlaws: The Extraordinary Lives of Mary Wollstonecraft & Mary Shelley. Random House.

Guston, David H., Ed Finn, and Jason Scott Robert, eds. Frankenstein: Annotated for Scientists, Engineers, and Creators of All Kinds. The MIT Press.

Hitchcock, Susan Tyler. Frankenstein: A Cultural History. W.W. Norton & Company.

Hoobler, Dorothy and Thomas. The Monsters: Mary Shelley and the Curse of Frankenstein. Little, Brown & Company.

Ito, Junji. Frankenstein. VIZ Media, LLC.

Levina, Marina, and Diem-My T. Bui, eds. Monster Culture in the 21st Century: A Reader. Bloomsbury Academic.

Mellor, Anne K. Mary Shelley: Her Life, Her Fiction, Her Monsters. Routledge.

Saadawi, Ahmed. Frankenstein in Baghdad. Penguin Books.

Shelley, Mary. Frankenstein. W.W. Norton & Company.

Shelley, Mary. Frankenstein: The 1818 Text. Penguin Books.

Wolfson, Susan J., and Ronald Levao, eds. The Annotated Frankenstein. Harvard University Press.

Wollstonecraft, Mary. A Vindication of the Rights of Woman. W.W. Norton & Company.

CPSIA information can be obtained
at www.ICGtesting.com
Printed in the USA
LVHW020009150523
746972LV00002B/303